THE MARRIAGE OF DR MARR

BY
LILIAN DARCY

20p

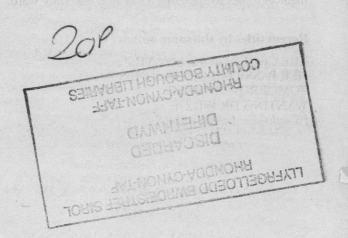

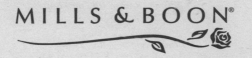

MILLS & BOON®

All the characters in this book have no existence outside the imagination of the author, and have no relation whatsoever to anyone bearing the same name or names. They are not even distantly inspired by any individual known or unknown to the author, and all the incidents are pure invention.

First published in Great Britain 2000
Harlequin Mills & Boon Limited,
Eton House, 18-24 Paradise Road, Richmond, Surrey TW9 1SR

© Lilian Darcy 2000

ISBN 0 263 82222 2

Set in Times Roman 10½ on 12 pt.
03-0003-52703

Printed and bound in Spain
by Litografia Rosés, S.A., Barcelona

CHAPTER ONE

I'M NOT looking forward to this, Dr Julius Marr thought to himself as he parked his dark red Saab in the narrow chink of space that had presented itself at last on Hickson Road between two very large four-wheel drives. I'm really not looking forward to this at all!

He fed the money-hungry meter as much as it would take, and noted that this would give him an excuse to leave after two hours...although surely Irene wouldn't want him for that long.

Meeting at the Sydney Theatre Company's Wharf restaurant had been her idea. 'I want to get away,' she had said distractedly on the phone. 'Somewhere I can *breathe*...clear my head.'

He had agreed... Perhaps he shouldn't have. He definitely preferred to keep their meetings businesslike these days, although once upon a time a long, elegant lunch with Irene would have put him on top of the world for the rest of the day.

Walking down the long approach to the restaurant along the mammoth boards of what had once been a working wharf, he conceded that it was a glorious setting, and a glorious day.

Early March in Sydney was technically autumn, but the sun was still hot overhead, everyone was in short sleeves and he and Irene would be able to eat out on the open-air terrace, with the water sparkling all around them. It would even sigh and swell directly beneath them, around the sturdy pier supports.

Irene would definitely be able to 'breathe'.

And, he conceded now with a pang of self-reproach, didn't she have good reason to feel stressed and pressured? Wasn't it good that she recognised the strain she was under and sought ways to replenish herself? Unwillingly, he felt a surge of real care and concern.

She wasn't here yet, he soon saw when he reached the restaurant. Uncharacteristically, he was a little late himself—blame the parking situation for that—and had already been preparing an apology. Instead, he said to the sleek, young waiter at the desk, 'I'm here to meet someone but she doesn't seem to have arrived. May I check that she has a reservation? Irene M...' He hesitated for a fraction of a second. What name was she using now? She had talked of going back to her maiden name even though the divorce would not be finalised for some months more.

Then, with his eyes as quick as always, he read it upside down in the reservation book and finished confidently, 'Irene Monaghan.'

So she *had* made the change! For some reason, the idea did not please him.

'Yes,' the waiter said. 'Here it is. One o'clock. And it's only just ten past, now.'

'Then I expect she had the same trouble with parking that I did,' Julius said with a smile.

'I can show you to your table,' the young man offered.

'Please, do. I don't expect she'll be long.'

She wasn't. Lateness had never been one of her faults. He sat down at one of the outside tables with his back to the water and could already see her hurrying down the long pier, her blonde hair swinging like a bell and her gait a little awkward in high heels. The boards were roughly finished, not designed for feminine extremes in footwear.

He also had the impression that she'd put on a little

weight lately. When had they last seen each other? The end of January? That long? It must be—about five weeks—although they'd spoken many times on the phone in the interim, of course, and communicated via e-mail.

'Sorry,' she said breathlessly at once, then she thumped a heavy briefcase onto the tabletop, hesitated for a moment and finally leaned across it to kiss him briefly on the mouth. He felt the tiniest touch of moisture from her tongue.

Taken quite by surprise, Julius responded clumsily, then blinked at her retreating face as she sat down. She looked flushed now. He reached for his metal-framed reading glasses and studied her more closely under the cover of putting them on. Yes, she definitely looked flustered. Self-conscious. Even a little defiant.

She was speaking again, just a little too quickly. 'Well, we have a lot to get through, as you know. So let's order, shall we? And get down to it?'

They didn't surface until their meal was well and truly finished, and their coffee-cups had been filled and emptied twice. A covert glance at his watch told Julius that he would risk a parking fine if he didn't make a move in the next five minutes, and he was about to say so when their waiter approached at Irene's signal and she asked, with a further hint of defiance, if she could have another glass of white wine.

Scarcely the moment, Julius realised, for him to announce his imminent departure. Mentally, he reviewed his plans for the rest of the day. He had deliberately kept the afternoon clear of commitments, but had hoped to have time for some much-needed tidying in his office and also a couple of house calls which weren't strictly necessary and wouldn't be billed, but which he thought were important as part of a GP's brief—Old Ron Daley who had terminal prostate cancer, Sally Kitchin who was at home with her brand-new triplets, and Stephanie Reid, who'd lost her mother to bowel cancer two months ago.

But with the necessary business of their meeting out of the way now, Irene clearly wanted to talk.

'And how have you *been*, Julius?' she asked him earnestly, her green eyes fixed on his face. 'I mean *really*? So much has changed...'

'Good,' he answered truthfully. 'Very good. I'm very happy about where I am at this point.' He had not had one minute's real regret about the major changes in his life over the past two years.

But he could tell at once that this was not the answer she wanted, and came in quickly to forestall further probing from her. 'But you don't need to hear about me. Tell me about *you*, Irene.'

She did, at length, emotionally, while taking rather large mouthfuls of her wine, and despite his underlying and very real concern he could not help being a reluctant listener. For a start, he had heard it all before, many times. More importantly, he didn't quite know—and she wasn't spelling it out—what it was that she wanted from him now and in the future. Just listening? Or action? Surely there was no action possible. It was simply a question of time and emotional courage on her part.

When she had finished and he had given what he hoped were the right replies, there was an awkward silence in which he felt the minutes ticking by and saw in his mind's eye the inexorable and menacing approach of a uniformed parking inspector towards his innocent and unsuspecting vehicle.

'Shall I ask for the bill?' he said gently at last, and received her assent.

Silence fell again, and he finally made himself ask, as he

should probably have asked at the beginning, 'How are the children?'

It was another half-hour before they finally left the restaurant.

He saw the buff envelope tucked beneath his windscreen wiper from forty metres away, knew at once what it was, and was thankful that he and Irene had separated as soon as they'd reached Hickson Road. She was taking a taxi across the Harbour Bridge to Chatswood and didn't need to know that her outpourings had cost him a hefty parking fine.

At heart, too, he didn't resent the three-hour lunch. His life had been bound up with Irene's for so long—over fourteen years. In such a comparatively small matter, he didn't need to let her down.

The lengthy meal did force a choice on him, though. Should he tidy the contents of that terrible desk which greeted him so reproachfully in his office at the Southshore Health Centre each morning? Or should he visit the three patients who were on his mind?

Five years ago there would have been no contest. The desk—it had been a different desk in a different place back then—would have won hands down. Today, the contest was equally one-sided. He chose at once to see his patients.

'It *is* thrush,' Julius told Sally Kitchin over the sound of crying babies and some potatoes boiling over on the stove. 'I'd better look at the other two and see if they've got it, too.'

'James is the only one that's fussing over his feeds.'

'Well, perhaps the others are just stoics because it does spread fairly easily. It can travel to their rectums, too, which also creates discomfort...'

He took crying Nicholas and gently probed his mouth

with a wooden tongue depressor. Yes, he had the same irregular white patches on tongue and cheek linings. Amelia was asleep, but he managed to look into her mouth as well, without waking her.

'I'll write you out for a couple of repeats on the prescription,' he told Sally, 'because you'll need it with three of them. Now, it's a lot like a paint. Yellow. And you just apply it directly to the patches. The boys don't have it in their little bottoms, so no need to do anything there unless something develops. Bring Amelia in if there's any sign of a rash or redness that looks unusual. And you must remember to put it on your nipples as well, before and after each feed.'

'Just what I need in my life on top of all this!' Sally groaned. 'Painting my nipples yellow!'

Julius laughed, but recognised that small complications like this could be the last straw for a twenty-seven year old first-time mother who was coping with triplets. Her husband was away at the moment, too. But Sally was a cheerful person and she'd wanted these babies desperately.

They were, in fact, the result of the difficult regime of fertility drugs she had been on for over a year before conceiving. Sometimes these drugs were actually *too* effective in promoting ovulation...

Now, though, in the thick of the first few difficult weeks at home, she had to be struggling.

'Your mum's gone back to Adelaide now, hasn't she?' he asked now, trying to get a firmer handle on her circumstances.

'Yes, this morning. I knew she couldn't stay for ever. She could only wangle three weeks off work. But still it was hard. *Is* hard! Michael isn't back from New Zealand for another month.'

Her voice cracked and she made a frantic attempt to

smile as she smeared tears from her eyes with the heel of her hand. For a minute the tears won, and she sniffed and sobbed and gulped. Then determination took over and she gave that valiant smile again.

I won't tell her what she's got in her hair, Julius decided to himself.

Actually, he didn't quite know *what* she had in her hair, but it was whitish, and it was making the long blonde strands stick stiffly together, and he could make an educated guess.

'He wants to earn an important promotion as soon as possible, you see,' Sally was saying firmly, 'so he had to make the trip. It's fine. It's good. With triplets, and me not working, we'll need the extra money he'll get. But I…just miss him.'

'That's tough, I know. And it would be tough even if he was here.'

'That's true,' Sally agreed.

'Would you like a child health nurse to come and see you?' Julius suggested. He took a pamphlet about the service out of his bag. 'They often have good strategies for managing babies' sleep patterns and all sorts of things. They can also put you in touch with other services and support groups.'

'Support groups? How do I get out of the house to a support group?' She laughed. 'No, I've got my own support group—a roster of friends taking turns to come for a couple of hours each day.'

'Is that enough?'

'No!' She gave a grimace. 'Of course not! Sorry… Don't I sound ungrateful? We struggled so long with infertility, and then three babies at once seemed like a miracle. It *is* a miracle! I love them! But I have to admit I'm exhausted!'

'It'll get easier. That's all I can promise,' he said, wishing there was more. 'Do try the child health nurse, and try the little ones on the thrush treatment as soon as you or one of your roster people can get to the chemist. Don't try to do too much. Forget about the state of the bathroom. Remember, physically you're still not fully recovered from the birth. By six weeks post-partum, when you come in for your check-up, you'll be starting to get a bit stronger.'

'Thanks, Dr Marr. I really appreciate you dropping in. Would you…um…like a cup of tea or something before you go?'

'No, I won't, I don't think,' he said. 'Thanks all the same.'

He had knocked back a similar offer from Ron Daley. It was half past five already and if he wanted to fit in Stephanie Reid at a decent hour he really should go…. He could, of course, leave her until another day, but he'd been wanting to see her for several weeks now, and he suspected that a postponement today would mean another over-long lapse of time. They were one receptionist short at the health centre at the moment, and the resultant pressure had twice meant, over the past week, that his wishes about slots left vacant in his schedule had been overlooked.

No, he decided, suddenly stubborn, he was definitely going to call in on Stephanie today. She lived very close to Sally. In fact, he realised as he looked at the street directory in his car, Stevie lived in the next street, and her back yard must almost share a fence with Sally's.

During the short drive around the block, he tried to pinpoint the exact date of Stephanie's mother's funeral, the time he'd last seen her. It had been a Friday, he remembered. Mid-January? The fifteenth? He thought so. And it was Friday today, the fifth of March. Seven weeks since she had sung so beautifully at the funeral, filling the church with the sound of words and music she had written herself.

He had known, in theory, that she could sing but had never dreamed that such a strong, beautiful sound could issue from that petite, red-headed form.

Julius had seen a lot of emotion from Stephanie Reid in the year or more that he'd known her. Laughter, fear, frustration, tears, and it all seemed to crystallise in his vivid memory of her singing. He wondered how he would find her today...

Oddly, it never even occurred to him that she might not be home, and when the bell pealed in vain as he stood outside the front door of her pretty little red-roofed Federation-era house, he felt the most absurd wash of disappointment ambush him out of nowhere. His mouth was suddenly parched, his neck muscles tense and he craved the tranquillity and warmth he remembered at the Reid house. And now he wasn't going to get the tea, the tranquillity or Stephanie!

Hell, that's showing my age! he thought, angry at himself. I'm only forty-two! Surely I'm not so set in my ways, so inflexible in my scheduling, that something like this can ruin the rest of my day?

Try as he may to talk himself out of it, however, the disappointment remained like a downward physical pull in his stomach, and he stumped quite grumpily off the tiled front porch and down the garden path to the gate.

Coming into the house from the back garden with her arms full of fresh-picked roses, Stevie heard the doorbell and hurried to answer it, the flowers still cradled in the crook of her left arm.

No one there.

Hang on, though. There was a tall, attractively dressed and vaguely familiar figure walking along the footpath at the front, past her blooming frangipani tree. With his back to her now, she couldn't work out who it was, but presumably he had been the man at the door.

'Excuse me,' she called, making good use of her singer's voice, and he turned. She recognised him now. 'Dr Marr!'

'You *are* home, then,' he said, coming back as she went down to meet him at the gate. There was a slightly accusatory note in his voice, and he was frowning darkly. She said quickly, showing him her roses, 'I was out in the back garden. Sorry, were you ringing and ringing?'

'Not long, really, I suppose,' he conceded, his tone gruff. He looked very dissatisfied about something.

She thought, Goodness, doctors *are* busy people, to get impatient about waiting a whole minute at someone's front door!

At heart, she couldn't resent his attitude, however. He'd been so good, so *very* good to Mum since starting at the Southshore Health Centre just over a year ago. She remembered the way he'd never rushed her mother's office visits, the way he would phone unexpectedly with a suggestion or question, often prefaced by the explanation, 'I've been reading up about...'

Stevie had soon realised that he hadn't only thought about her mother in the few minutes immediately before and after each appointment.

Then, in those first two horrendous weeks of this past January, when Mum had lived beyond her diagnosis of terminal cancer by only two weeks, he'd helped so much. If he was as good as that to everyone, then, yes, every minute of his time *was* precious.

'Do come in,' she told him warmly, feeling her gratitude in full measure all over again.

What a tall, capable figure he made, standing there at the gate! The sort of doctor who instantly inspired trust. Dark hair, mobile, intelligent face, *lovely* taste in clothes, with that impeccably fitted grey-brown shirt and darker matching pants. Mum had commented more than once on Dr Marr's attractive clothes, and Stevie had enjoyed the fact that a little thing like that had still given her mother pleasure. Silly to be *grateful* to a doctor for dressing well, but she was, all the same.

'Would you like tea or coffee…or a drink?'

But he frowned and looked at his watch, and Stevie wondered at once if she'd overstepped the bounds. She suddenly felt that she had, and didn't understand what had prompted the impulse. Something was different today…

'I'm sure you don't have time… I know you must be busy,' she began, offering him an easy way out. She was quite surprised to find that he didn't take it.

'No,' he said slowly, 'I'm not busy. Not now. A drink would be very nice.'

'Let me deal with these roses, then,' she said, turning towards the house.

'They're lovely.'

'All Mum's work, as is most of the garden. I helped a lot, of course, but I was only following orders. I'm rather new to being in charge, and I doubt I'll have her touch for them.'

They entered the house and Julius followed her back to the kitchen, which still caught some sun from its north-facing windows. Stupidly, she felt flustered in a way she'd never felt with Dr Marr before and she realised that it was because he wasn't here to see Mum. They didn't have her health to talk about. They didn't have her here with them to carry the conversation.

As if she had acted as our chaperone…which is quite absurd! she thought.

Stevie herself was almost sinfully healthy. She trotted dutifully along to the health centre once a year for her Pap smear, but even then didn't insist on seeing the family physician for such a small detail. Other than that, she couldn't remember when she'd last been sick enough to need a doctor. She had never, in any sense of the word, been Julius Marr's patient at all.

Still cradling the roses, which provided a welcome camouflage for her sudden awkwardness, she reached for a glass vase on the mantel above the old kitchen fireplace, in a hurry to get the job done. Dr Marr didn't want to stand around, waiting for his drink. Very probably he'd only accepted her offer out of politeness, and out of the same desire she had now to smooth this kind visit of his and make it pleasant.

He was tying off the loose ends, she knew, making sure that the bereaved daughter of his patient was coping with her grief and moving on.

Which she was, and she would tell him so.

Thinking too much about this and not enough about her roses, she simply flung them into the vase and was rewarded by a sharp thorn giving her a long, shallow tear across the stretch of skin between left thumb and forefinger. It stung and she gasped unwillingly. Blood was welling in a streak across her fair skin.

'What have you done?' said Dr Marr, taking her hand and watching the red droplets rise. 'Bad luck!'

His fingers were warm, dry and very pleasant against her skin, and she felt an odd heat rising up her arm that had nothing to do with her fresh injury. It was ludicrous! What would he think if he knew?

'I was careless,' she said, and snatched her hand away, picked up the vase of flowers and went to the sink to fill them with water. 'It's nothing.'

'Wash it, at least.'

Dutifully, she held her hand beneath the tap, then heard him add, 'And are you up to date on your tetanus?'

She laughed. 'Probably not. I don't suppose I've had one since I was a teenager, which is twenty years ago. But you don't seriously think...'

'Not from a clean scratch by a rose thorn, no,' he agreed. 'But if you're going to keep gardening, you should.'

'Really?' She was a little startled.

'I gave your mother one last year for the same reason—don't you remember?'

'Sorry...'

'Tetanus lives in the soil. Ring up next week and make an appointment.'

'OK. Thanks.'

'I'm sorry. That wasn't a lecture.'

'I didn't take it as one.'

'Good.' He smiled, and once again the effect was new and startling.

'So...' she managed. Their drinks. And why couldn't she be more graceful about all this? Why did she feel so flustered?

Most importantly, what did one offer a doctor? Sherry immediately sprang to mind as the appropriate choice, but somehow that reeked of aging Victorian spinsters, Agatha Christie novels and the days when doctors motored from patient to patient in their Bentleys and could carry the whole of Western medical knowledge in their black leather bags. She would give the distinct impression that she was old-fashioned.

No, Stevie decided firmly, I am *not* going to offer him sherry!

'Beer?' she suggested, strongly suspecting there was none in the house. 'Wine? Gin and tonic?'

'A gin and tonic sounds nice.'

'And would you like to sit in the garden?'

It was a delightful setting—white-painted wrought-iron chairs and table placed amongst roses and lavender and hydrangeas, as well as semitropical hibiscus and bougainvillea, and native Australian bottle-brush, boronia and flowering gum. Not everything was in flower, but everything was green and lush and it was late enough that the sun threw long, cool shadows.

The only pity of it was that for a good minute or more—after they had both agreed how nice it was to sit here and how good it was that Mum had managed to garden for a good hour on most days, almost till the end, with some assistance from Stevie and a professional gardener—she couldn't think of a thing to say. She found, furthermore, that a minute of silence in the company of a man you didn't really know very well could seem like a very long time indeed.

She stared down into her drink, as if there was something absolutely fascinating about the way the tiny bubbles rose in the clear liquid, and then took a good big gulp of it, absolutely determined that it would let her relax.

Meanwhile, he was the one to find voice, as he shifted to uncross and re-cross his long legs. 'Does your garden back on to Sally and Michael Kitchins', by any chance?'

'Oh, you know the Kitchins?'

'She's a patient, and so are the new triplets.'

'I haven't met them yet—although I've heard them—but, yes, in answer to your question, our gardens meet at the corner. We don't have any fence in common, but we chat while we're hanging out our washing. I've heard several reports on the babies from Sally's mother, who's been hanging out a clothesline full of nappies every day.'

'Her mother has gone back to Adelaide now, unfortunately, just this morning.'

'Hmm, I can imagine what that means for Sally! I must let her known I'm available to help.'

She had spoken the words quite unselfconsciously, Julius noted. She was sipping her drink and relaxing into her seat as much as wrought iron would let her. Watching her, he was given the strong impression that her drink must be the most delicious thing in the world, and this garden setting akin to paradise. He was beginning to realise that everything was this way for her—to be lived and experienced and *felt* to the fullest.

It reminded him of the stated professional purpose of his visit—to check on the well-being of a bereaved carer—and he changed the subject far too abruptly and asked, 'What are you going to do now, Stephanie?'

'Please call me Stevie, as you always used to,' she blurted, which didn't answer his question.

'Stevie, then,' he agreed, realising that this was what he still *did* call her, to himself.

'You mean…' she laughed a little nervously '…With my life, don't you? Not with this evening?'

'With your life, yes,' he answered, well aware that his lack of subtlety bordered on the tactless.

'Is that why you've come?' Oh, what a stupid thing to say! Stevie groaned inwardly.

'I mean, I appreciate that you took the time,' she went on, more sensibly and carefully, willing her heightened colour to fade. 'I'm taking things slowly. I've decided to stay in the house as it's mine, now. I'll keep on singing with Lizzy in the Kitchen, of course, because I love that, but we're not professional enough to get more than pocket money for it, so I will need a job. Dad's work pension stopped when Mum died, you see, and my solicitor says— Not that you're remotely interested in my finances, of course.'

What is *wrong* with me? I'm burbling!

'What sort of job?' he cut in.

Stevie spread her hands and smiled, glad of the interruption. 'My curriculum vitae won't be very impressive! I did a year of nursing, but that was fifteen years ago, and then I dropped out for…for personal reasons. Then, of course, Mum was diagnosed with multiple sclerosis, and I started secretarial temping because the flexible hours meant I could be on call during her bad periods.

'When she started getting worse I worked on a volunteer basis part time for a charity, doing phone-answering, book-keeping and fund-raising. About five years ago I stopped work altogether, so I hope my skills haven't dated too much. If necessary, I'll retrain, spend a few months learning more advanced computer skills. There's enough of a cushion, financially, to give me until next year.'

Oh, just stop, Stevie! Edit yourself a little!

'And it doesn't bother you to have it so uncertain?'

Was that a criticism? She wasn't sure, but sought to put a positive light on her future nonetheless, and said, meaning it, 'For me it's not *what* I do but how I do it. My singing and song-writing with the band gives me a lot of creative satisfaction, so I don't need to find those things through a job. I'd like something busy and people-oriented. I don't mind hard work. I can cope with pressure, I think, as well as routine.'

And if I don't stop now I'll sound as if I'm at a job interview here and now.

'You should have no trouble, I expect,' he answered. 'Even in this economic climate. Someone mature, steady, well educated, well spoken, enthusiastic…' He stopped, then echoed her own thought aloud, with a comic twist, 'And the Julius Marr Employment Agency would be happy to take you on as a client.'

She laughed. 'But what's your commission?'

'Fifteen per cent of everything you earn for ever afterwards,' he replied, as quick as a flash. 'Six-month contract, open to renewal at my discretion but not yours.'

'I'll shop around, I think,' she answered in the same vein. 'I somehow suspect there might be a better deal elsewhere.'

'Hmm… Perhaps that's why I don't have many clients.'

Stevie laughed again, then there was a small silence, which slowly lengthened…and lengthened some more. She had enjoyed that bit of silliness, and that and the drink had now relaxed her too much, if that were possible. Looking covertly across at him, she thought again that it was as if she were seeing him for the first time today.

She had never noticed before, for example, that he was so…no, not good-looking… He wasn't, exactly. But he had such a presence. Tall, well built, well dressed, confident and intelligent. She'd always thought of him as Mum's GP, the man who had replaced Dr Crane at the health centre.

She had never struggled for something to say because there had always been questions to ask about Mum. She had never wondered about his personal circumstances because, when he had answered those many medical questions of hers, she had always been too preoccupied with the answers to wonder much about the man who had given them.

Now she was suddenly full of curiosity. What had he done before coming to Southshore? Did he like being a doctor? What else did he do? What family did he have in Sydney? Was he married? He'd never mentioned anything about his personal life, but that was very probably because she had never expressed an interest, never given him a chance.

Half a dozen questions crowded to her lips but she didn't feel confident in asking any of them in case he should regard it as an invasion of privacy and an inappropriate crossing of his professional boundaries. It was exactly that, she realised, disturbed. There was no good reason for her to *want* to know such things about him.

He must have experienced it more than once—lonely female patients getting just a little nosy and a little too familiar. She would burn with shame if she did anything to make him class her in such a category.

What on earth can I say? There must be something! This is horrible...

He must have thought so, too. He finished his drink with indecent speed then stood up. Stevie immediately did the same, because really he was just too tall to converse with comfortably from a sitting position, even if she did manage to come up with something suitable and a tiny bit interesting.

She considered offering him another drink, to give herself a chance to redeem the occasion, but they'd already covered all the obvious conversation points and she was afraid that any more silence would be just too embarrassing.

He was beginning to look embarrassed now, in fact, as he reached to put his empty glass on the table.

'I'll take it,' Stevie said quickly, and their fingers touched as she did so. Again, she felt an odd sensation of warmth radiating outwards from their point of contact and moved her hand abruptly. He had wonderful hands. Strong, but not beefy, with the clean, square-cut nails she would expect of a doctor.

They both began to edge away from the table and she realised that it was up to her to take the situation in hand and find the right way to close this not entirely pleasant interlude. She was horribly disappointed in herself, feeling that she'd lost an unexpectedly precious opportunity to...

What? She didn't even know. And very possibly she

would not see this man again. This realisation reminded her of something that *did* need to be said.

'Thank you for caring so much about Mum,' she said seriously. 'I'm not sure that I've said it before, and I ought to have done, months ago.'

'I didn't come to be thanked,' he told her. 'I came to see how you were.'

'I know,' she replied honestly, 'but somehow it's not as easy to thank you for that, so I'm thanking you for Mum, instead.'

'I think you just *have* thanked me for "that".'

'I suppose I have. Well, I may as well do it formally, then. Thank you, Dr Marr, for caring about how I am.'

He hesitated for a moment, then answered her, 'All part of the service at Southshore Health Centre.'

She privately doubted that every doctor at the health centre would be able to make the same claim, but didn't say so. They were both starting to walk towards the back door, and to cut the business of his departure short she said aloud, 'It would be easier, Dr Marr, if I took you round through the side gate.'

'Yes,' he said. 'All right.'

He drove off a few minutes later, while she stood on the front porch and watched. A brief visit. Kind, casual. Strangely, though, having felt fairly contented before his unexpected arrival, she felt quite flat after he had gone. The feeling lasted most of the weekend, too, and her grief for Mum, which had begun to reach a quiet, constant, *patient* sort of stage, surged again and was not assuaged by the church line-dancing social where Lizzy in the Kitchen played on Saturday night.

No one else in the five-woman country music band lived alone. Three of them were married and one was divorced with teenage children.

I'm lonely, Stevie realised. It's time I did something about that job!

It's definitely time I did something about that desk! Julius thought again as he stopped in briefly at the health centre to pick up some papers.

The papers were not actually in the desk, which was perhaps fortunate as it might otherwise have taken him some minutes to locate them. Retrieving them from a shelf, he looked at the desk in a dispassionate sort of way and the sight of it confirmed his initial impression.

Yes, it was really terrible. The second drawer couldn't shut properly at all, it was so crammed. Even the top of it needed some attention.

And did he intend to do anything about it now? No!

He was feeling distinctly grumpy again—grumpier than he had felt when he'd been about to give up on Stephanie Reid answering her doorbell. This time he found it less easy to analyse the reason for his mood. A few minutes' thought, as he checked that he'd turned off all the lights and left the building as it should be, brought the understanding that, again, he was disappointed.

Disappointed in Stephanie herself.

Or perhaps it was me...

In the past he had found her so easy to talk to, had liked and admired her and hadn't made any attempt to conceal this warmth as it was entirely professional in nature.

It would have been hard for a doctor *not* to like someone who had done such an incredible job of nursing his patient, who had appeared to have given no thought to the fact that it had been a sacrifice, who had bent over backwards to make sure that her mother had still been able to enjoy her favourite pastimes as much as had been medically possible, and who nonetheless had somehow managed to have a vibrant life of her own, which had meant that when he'd met Stevie there had always been something to say.

Today, though, their ease with each other, which he had always taken for granted, had been patchy at best. Our relationship has changed, he realised. There's no reason for us ever to meet after today.

An uncomfortable sense of loss began to nag at him and, although he had far too much else to think about, he found that he couldn't dismiss her from his mind...

CHAPTER TWO

FIFTEEN advertisements circled in the classifieds, twelve phone calls made, three business schools contacted to find out about their short computer courses, six more phone calls still on her list to explore various other possibilities…

By ten-thirty on Monday morning, the last thing Stevie wanted as she grabbed a coffee was to hear the phone ringing. No one had yet expressed an urgent desire to interview her, but could this possibly be the first such somewhat daunting phone call now?

It wasn't. It was Dr Marr, whom she had been thinking about in an unsatisfactory sort of way all weekend.

He had a nice phone voice, deep and just a little burred, but it was a bit unsettling to hear it when she'd been dwelling on him so much, and she blurted guiltily, 'I haven't had a chance yet to make an appointment to get that tetanus booster, Dr Marr. I'm sorry.'

She didn't stop to realise that he would scarcely call about something as trivial as that.

'What?' he answered distractedly. 'Oh! Yes! You should! But I wasn't ringing about—'

'No… Of course you weren't!'

'No, it occurred to me, you see, that you ought to come in and be interviewed for a receptionist's position we have going here.'

Stevie panicked at once, barely heard his explanation about what the job involved, and was on the point of telling him that she couldn't come in because she was quite positive that she didn't have any suitable clothes when she realised that that hardly added up to what she had told him the other day about being able to cope with pressure. And what exactly was he saying?

'Do you think you could possibly come in this morning? I'm on the interview panel and, frankly, we haven't been too impressed by the other candidates. The two we've liked best so far are both unable to start for several weeks. I've been thinking about you all weekend and kicking myself that I didn't put two and two together and make the suggestion on Friday.'

'I can be there whenever you want me,' she told him firmly, ignoring the issue of the clothes. Suddenly, in the space of two minutes, she wanted this job quite badly and didn't bother to stop and ask herself why.

'Well, we were hoping to wind up the interviews by lunchtime,' he said, 'and we have a gap at eleven forty-five…'

'I'll see you then,' she promised blithely, and put down the phone.

The thing was, she really *didn't* have any clothes! The plain grey dress she had worn to her mother's funeral held too many memories now. The array of Western outfits she wore to sing with Lizzy in the Kitchen were clean and smart and pretty, but you couldn't wear a fringed satin shirt, studded jeans and elaborately tooled leather boots to a job interview, even when you did know someone on the panel.

She also had two simple and elegant silk dresses, one dark green, one black, which she wore on the rare occasions when she went out in the evenings, but bare shoulders and a hint of cleavage were even less suitable than fringes and studs.

At a quarter past eleven, after madly gathering up a folder of old job references, typing certificates, exam result printouts, her first-year nursing results and, for good measure, her birth certificate, she headed out of the door still dressed in shorts and a T-shirt, with pantihose and heeled shoes—black—in a bag, and sketchy make-up and hair.

Now, there was a clothing boutique just a couple of blocks from the health centre...

'Do you have any petite-sized suits?' she gabbled at the sales assistant.

'A few, yes.'

'Can I try them on?'

'All of them? Without looking at them on the rack?'

'I'm in a hurry, you see...'

She arrived at the health centre at precisely eleven forty-four, clad in a navy linen-blend suit and a cream silk blouse, and exchanged her running shoes for her heels just outside the front door.

I'm obviously the one they want, she decided firmly. Resourceful, speedy, well groomed...sort of!

And, unfortunately, breathless. They were running on time, too, so she was still panting a little when ushered in to Julius Marr's office.

Under the circumstances the interview went well, she considered. Dr Gareth Searle, who directed Southshore Health Centre, asked her several questions about her mother's multiple sclerosis and she answered them thoughtfully, realizing that he wanted to learn about her attitude to modern health care and its professional providers.

Ros Reynolds, the office manager, asked her about her experience with various aspects of office work and office equipment, and about her willingness to work odd hours sometimes when clinics and classes were held in the late afternoon or evening.

Stevie said that, yes, irregular hours were fine and told the truth about what she was familiar with and what she wasn't.

Dr Marr didn't say much at all, just listened and nodded with his fingertips pressed together. Just before the interview ended, another woman popped in to say, 'Your twelve-fifteen candidate has just rung to cancel, Dr Searle, so Ms Reid is the last.'

Accordingly, when they were finished with her, everyone stood up and the two doctors left the room. Stevie was about to do the same when Ros Reynolds held her back and said in a conspiratorial whisper, 'I must tell you, there's a price tag sticking out of your skirt.'

'Oh, no!'

'Don't worry. I don't think the doctors noticed, but there are some scissors here on Dr Marr's desk. Gee, he needs to tidy it, doesn't he? Do let me cut it off for you!'

'With pleasure! This is what comes of trying to buy a suit in fifteen minutes!'

'Oh, my goodness, did you buy it this morning, after Dr Marr rang you at half past ten?' In her fifties, with beautifully coiffed dark hair, Ros Reynolds was immaculately groomed herself.

'Yes,' Stevie said. 'Perhaps that was foolish but I really had nothing else to—'

'Foolish! Love, it's quite impressive! If you're that efficient with your time, then you get *my* vote! Although it's the doctors who have the final say.'

'Thanks.' Stevie laughed. 'And thank you for telling me about the tag!'

Ros cut it off and looked at the price with raised eyebrows and a cheeky expression. 'A good discount, too! And it looks lovely on you.'

Ros would be nice to work with, Stevie decided. She was soon able to conclude, on the basis of similar evidence, that Dr Searle would be nice to work with, too. 'Ah, good,' he said, encountering her in the corridor just beyond the large waiting area. 'You've cut the tag off your skirt, I see.'

Stevie stifled an exclamation of dismay.

'Don't worry, little mate,' he assured her in an elder brother sort of way, 'I don't think the others noticed. It only showed when you sat down. But I was about to offer you some scissors.' He flourished them.

She didn't see Dr Marr again that morning and, after filling in some forms under Ros's guidance, left the centre with the information that they hoped to reach a decision that day.

Dr Marr rang at six that evening. 'You've got the job,' he said. 'And if you could possibly start this week...'

'Wednesday, if you like,' Stevie agreed, wisely realising that she needed tomorrow for a second, more leisurely shopping expedition to buy work clothes.

She was happy and relieved about the news. Some more enquiries on the phone this afternoon had not been encouraging. Most computer courses were not cheap, and she'd just missed one enrolment deadline.

'Er, by the way,' Dr Marr said now, 'you may want to cut off the price tag on your suit...very *attractive* suit...before you wear it again. I don't think the others noticed, fortunately,' he added kindly. 'It only showed when you sat down, but I thought you'd want to know.'

'Th-thanks, Dr Marr,' Stevie answered him weakly.

After putting down the phone, Julius wondered if it had been the right thing to mention that price tag. He'd obviously embarrassed her, and yet it would scarcely have been chivalrous to let her remain in ignorance. He had hoped to waylay her immediately after the interview, but an important phone call had been waiting for him and by the time he'd finished with it she had gone.

Unwillingly, he smiled. There had been something typically spirited and gallant about her this morning, arriving in such a hurry, fielding their questions so seriously and energetically, and yet all the time looking so petite and almost doll-like with her small build and fine, flawless fair skin that you could easily have thought that the price tag on her skirt had applied to her.

Stephanie, the secretary doll, hand-painted porcelain, $99.95.

She probably wouldn't thank him for comparing her to a doll, with all its connotations of passivity and helplessness. She was the very opposite, from what he knew of her. Such qualities would not do in the job either. He had had to stick his neck out a little for her. Gareth had had doubts because of the length of time she had been out of the professional workforce and the fact that a medical practice was new to her. Ros had been confident, however, and he would thank her for that.

Should I have pushed for her like that? he wondered. It'll backfire on me if she doesn't measure up. Was I an idiot to risk such a thing?

He didn't have time to give the issue full consideration. The phone rang, and it was Irene, still in her office, with a barrage of questions which could easily have waited. He answered them, however, while wondering in the back of his mind where Kyle and Lauren were. Still in after-school care at this hour?

He had to work hard to convince himself that it wasn't his concern, and that brought his thoughts back to the subject of Stephanie Reid once more. He had no obligation at all towards her, yet he'd just gone well out of his way to create an ongoing connection between them.

And, having quite deliberately schooled himself in self-awareness over the past few years, he was starting to have

a very good idea why. The new knowledge did not please
him…

Whatever Stevie's questions about how her relationship
with Julius Marr had now changed, he was definitely a
friend to her that first day at Southshore Health Centre.

Thanks to her shopping expedition yesterday, she was
very suitably dressed in tailored taupe linen pants, cinna-
mon-brown leather court shoes and a matching blouse, and
she'd made very certain that all tags, labels, stickers and
pins of any description had been safely removed.

She was distinctly rusty when it came to office routine,
and she had not worked for a medical practice before. There
was so much to remember! Patient files filled a whole room.
The telephone console had fifteen lines. The computer simply refused to perform at all if she didn't key in all its
commands in precisely the right way.

Ros Reynolds was extremely patient. Cathy Hong, also
at the reception desk today, got her out of trouble at least
six times, and even the patients were very supportive.

'Shouldn't you write my name on the specimen jar so
you'll know it's mine?' suggested a white-haired pensioner
who, just a quarter of an hour earlier, had taken eleven
minutes to search her bag for her Medicare card.

By lunchtime Stevie had a raging headache, had to think
for some seconds before she could remember whether Q
came before or after R in the alphabet, and was wondering
whether it was at all possible that any of her mistakes might
actually kill someone. It seemed unlikely, but was an
alarming idea nonetheless.

She had just begun to envisage a frightening scenario in
which Dr Searle was prevented from administering emergency heart massage to a Mr Macintosh because Stevie had
filed his file in amongst the Ms instead of with the Macs,

which all came first, when Dr Marr emerged from his office and announced cheerfully that he was taking her to lunch.

'You look a bit overwhelmed,' he said when she had retrieved her bag and was accompanying him across the street.

'More than a bit!' she confessed.

They both carried umbrellas because it was raining. Real Sydney rain, it was—thunderously heavy, plunging from thick, woolly clouds, so that the streets were already deep in water, although only five minutes ago they had been dry. It wasn't cold, though, just pleasantly fresh and cool.

'It's your first day,' Dr Marr reminded her gently as they attained the comparative dryness of the kerb.

There was a café serving light meals tucked in amongst a group of shops, and once they were inside he led the way directly to a quiet table at the back. A waitress was just coming past and he got her attention with one commanding yet far from overbearing lift of his finger.

He asked for a glass of water, then waved her away before Stevie could say anything, which was a pity because she'd have ordered one for herself.

But the water appeared less than a minute later, and Dr Marr produced a small foil packet, then tore it open to shake forth a white tablet. 'Here,' he said. 'For your headache.' He slid the water towards her as well.

Her jaw dropped weakly. 'How did you know?'

'You've got it written across your forehead,' he said with his slow smile, 'in shimmering red letters.'

'Oh, dear! That bad!' She didn't protest about the tablet, but downed it quickly with a gulp of water then finished off the whole glass.

'Now, please, don't just pick a plain ham sandwich to eat!' he said next.

'I was going to,' she confessed. 'Perhaps you'd like to prescribe something instead?'

'Quiche and salad,' he answered promptly. 'Followed by a very large, very pink and very sticky iced bun, and an even larger pot of tea.'

'Oh…' she said, surprised. 'That *does* sound good! I feel better already!'

He ordered lasagne and salad for himself, and while they waited for the meal to arrive he told her some details of his morning in a chatty kind of way, which meant Stevie didn't realise until he'd finished that, in fact, he'd been briefing her, clarifying the routine, warning her about the sort of problems she might encounter.

When her plate of steaming cheese and herb quiche and crisp, imaginative salad was set down in front of her, she blurted, 'Why did I get this job, Dr Marr? Because you felt sorry for me?'

His eyes widened in amazement. 'Why on earth should I feel sorry for you?'

'Well, because I was obviously going to have trouble finding anything through the usual channels.'

'Have trouble? We snapped you up before anyone else could get hold of you!'

'I really can't see myself as much of a professional prize,' she countered. 'Especially after this morning!'

'Garbage! In all the right respects, you were ideal. For a start, you went to school in an era when people still learned how to spell and write a legible hand. We had a very nice girl in her mid-twenties a few months ago who fortunately left to study horticulture. She couldn't spell anything longer than ''cat'', couldn't read her own handwriting half the time and, of course, neither could anyone else. Neither are you likely to leave without notice in two weeks' time to go off overseas with some unsuitable boyfriend, like our last candidate did.'

'No?' she countered indignantly, feeling that she was quite as capable of having an unsuitable boyfriend as any other woman.

'No!' Julius insisted. 'No matter how unsuitable he was, you'd definitely give decent notice!'

She laughed.

'And,' he continued more seriously, 'you have years' personal experience of nursing a loved one with a complex and chronic illness, so you know exactly how it feels to be on the other side of the fence, and at the front desk that can come in handy.'

'But if I can't get a grip on the phones and the computer and the files...'

'Stevie, you're an intelligent woman,' he said, almost sternly now. 'I've spent enough time with you in the course of your mother's illness to know that. You can learn files and phones in a week. To learn empathy and reliability and common sense takes a lot longer.'

'Yes...' she agreed slowly, 'I see what you're saying.'

'Good.'

He watched her, his head tilted a little to one side, and suddenly she felt self-conscious. 'Well, this looks delicious,' she managed. 'I'd better get stuck into it.'

He began to eat too, and she studied him covertly, taking in the details of his face and form. Not for the first time. She was struggling with this unexpected new impression of him which had started last week, still trying to find a safe place to put it. He wasn't, she supposed, what most people would consider a handsome man. His face was too long, his mouth too wide and his jaw too square and jutting.

His eyes, though, were extraordinary. She'd never really noticed his eyes before, perhaps because they were often disguised by wire-framed glasses. Grey eyes…a dark, slatey grey, fringed by long lashes.

He didn't have his glasses on now, and she could tell that he was long-sighted because he narrowed his gaze just a little and lifted his head back every time he looked at her. It was an appealing gesture somehow.

'Do you have any performances with your band this weekend?' he asked.

'No, we don't,' she answered, pleased that he'd remembered and had expressed an interest, even though he was probably just making small talk. 'We're practising, though, on Friday night.'

'Do you play an instrument? Or just sing?'

'Just sing, mostly. Occasionally I whack a bongo drum or ring a bell, but that's about the extent of my instrumental virtuosity these days.'

'And are bells and bongos usual in a country music band?'

She laughed. 'We like our moments of originality.'

They talked this way for another half hour, while the rain still pelted down outside. The quiche and salad were delicious and really hit the spot, and the bun and tea were so home-like that she felt as cosy as a cat and didn't even notice her headache disappearing.

When he asked for the bill it was like having to get out of a warm bed in an icy room, but the thought of the afternoon ahead didn't daunt and dismay her as it done an hour ago. His company, his cosseting and his confidence in her had nourished her thoroughly.

Crossing the street back to the health centre, she realised he was so much taller than she was that the rain from the points of his umbrella dripped onto the very top of hers, and he was broad enough that when a gust of wind cut through the rain to reach them she scarcely felt it, sheltered as she was by his body.

Her awareness of his warm bulk beside her was delicious, as was the sound of his slightly burred voice warning, 'Careful! There's a puddle as big as a swimming pool just in front of you.' Although she didn't see it coming then, she was to say to herself many times later on, with a twist in her heart, Perhaps loving him started from that moment...

The afternoon was far better than the morning. Her headache did not return, the alphabet stayed in its correct order in her brain, and she only cut off one person in mid-sentence on the phone. Even the sequence of computer commands was starting to stick.

And at half past five she was able to be of real use, even in her own over-critical eyes.

The health centre was busy at that time of day. Several school-age children and their parents and siblings filled the waiting area, and three of the five doctors currently on duty, including Dr Marr, were running behind. It wasn't the best moment for a new patient to arrive without an appointment, but Stan Truesdale wasn't thinking of that.

'I want to see a doctor,' he said in a quavering and querulous voice. 'I'm having trouble with my waterworks.'

Two children overheard this and giggled, but Mr Truesdale didn't notice.

Stevie knew the routine by now and asked him, 'Do you have an appointment?'

No.

'And have you been here before?'

No, again.

In theory that was all right. Like the accident and emergency department of the large hospital with which it was so closely affiliated, Southshore Health Centre took all comers, but in the last half-hour of a busy day…

'We'll fit you in as soon as we can, then,' Stevie promised him.

'Can't he see me straight away?' the old man asked.

'I'm afraid not,' Stevie answered patiently, forbearing to point out that it might well be a she, as two of the five doctors today were female. Actually… 'Would you prefer to see a man, then?' she asked him quietly, not wanting those giggling children to find further cause for mirth in this patient.

He didn't look well nourished, he definitely wasn't well dressed and he more than definitely smelled. He didn't need his feelings hurt as well!

'You mean it's a *woman doctor*?' he rasped, in horror at this.

'We have five doctors on. Three of them are male,' she explained. 'If you'd like to see one of them, then you certainly can, but it may mean a longer wait.'

'I don't want to wait at all,' he repeated. 'I want to be seen straight away.'

Stevie didn't press the point. 'Would you give me your Medicare card and fill in this form, then?' she said. 'And then give us a specimen?'

She produced a jar and handed it to him, and he seemed satisfied with this apparent progress, although Stevie privately intended to have him wait his turn as he should. When he'd sat down with clipboard and pen to fill in his medical history form, she said as much to Ros Reynolds and received a confirmatory nod.

'Yes,' the health centre manager said. 'You have to resist the temptation to start triaging the walk-ins. We're not nurses. If they do need urgent attention they must go to Accident and Emergency across at the hospital, where there *is* a proper triage nurse who'll assess them and jump them ahead of the queue if it's warranted. Has he said what's wrong?'

'Trouble with his "waterworks",' she said.

'Along with about forty per cent of Australian men over forty-five years of age,' Ros answered.

'I thought you said you weren't a nurse.' Stevie was impressed at the statistic, quoted so confidently.

'We pick things up,' Ros commented. 'Actually, I do read all the pamphlets we have here for patient information.'

'I should do the same, perhaps.'

'Yes, it helps to have an overview, and a bit of lay knowledge. I've been in medical administration for twenty years now, and sometimes things still take me by surprise!'

She gave a laugh and disappeared back into the file room, while Stevie made a mental note to take home a sheaf of patient information pamphlets that weekend. That year of nursing she'd done now seemed such a very long time ago...

Mr Truesdale had finished filling out his form. He put it on the desk in front of Stevie and then stood there, waiting impatiently. She glanced at the form and saw that it seemed to be fully completed. Whether it was completed *accurately* was another matter. There was a long line of quavery yet emphatic ticks in the 'No' column that ran down half a page, indicating that he'd led a life of enviable health. No allergies, no high blood pressure, no hospitalisations, no heart trouble...

The list went on, and when she saw that he'd even put a tick for 'No' in answer to, 'Have you ever had any urinary problems?' she realised that the form was so unreliable as to be useless.

Dr Marr's appointments were the least backed up. I'll

send Mr Truesdale in to him, she decided. And let him know that he ought to probe pretty carefully for the real details.

Aloud, she reminded Mr Truesdale that he needed to produce a specimen. It wasn't really her job to suggest this, but he seemed so impatient, and since, given his stated complaint, she was quite sure that Dr Marr would want one from him, it seemed the best idea. She pointed the way across the peach coloured tiles of the reception area to the pleasant and private patient bathroom.

He shuffled off in that direction, looking glum and uneasy. Glancing at his form again, she saw that his birth date had been written as 10 March, 1933. Her first thought was that he was younger than he looked. She'd have pegged him as in his mid-seventies. Her second was that March the tenth was today, which either meant that he was more confused than he seemed, or today was his birthday.

I'll ask him about it when he comes out, she decided. Poor man!

Meanwhile, time wasn't standing still. Two more patients had presented themselves for their appointments and she had to make an imprint of their Medicare cards on her little machine. Someone else's file had accidentally got moved to the wrong pile.

And now Mr Truesdale was back, with an empty jar.

'I can't,' he said. 'Feels like I should, but I can't. So I s'pose there's no point in seeing him today. I'll come back another time. You're not going to charge me for this, are you?'

'We're not going to charge you for anything, Mr Truesdale, but—'

'Excuse me,' interrupted a frantic young mother. 'My daughter's about to be sick. Where's the bathroom?'

'See the door over there?' Stevie began, but it was too

late, and by the time she'd got paper towelling, a bucket of water, disinfectant and a mop, Mr Truesdale had shuffled his way out the door.

'Let him go,' advised brisk young Anna Lewis, who was also working the front desk now. 'He'll come back if it's important.'

'I suppose so,' Stevie agreed. She could still see him through the glass doors, waiting to cross Avoca Street, where all the gutters still ran and the cars sent up impressive splashes, although the clouds were clearing now.

He looked neither comfortable nor happy, and she thought back on what he had said— 'Feels like I should, but I can't.'

Mum said exactly the same thing, Stevie remembered, a couple of years ago when she had that sudden exacerbation of her symptoms, and— She didn't stop long enough to complete the thought. Barging past a startled Anna, she left the front desk, went round through the file room and out the staff door, crossed a waiting room full of patients and ran out to the street.

'Mr Truesdale!'

At last the heavy traffic had cleared enough to let him through and he had reached the far kerb. 'Mr Truesdale, wait!'

But he didn't hear her, and the lights down at the intersection of Anzac Parade were green again.

I can't let him go, she thought.

He was heading up in the direction of the Nine Ways, and she followed him on her own side of the street, keeping pace with him and still waiting for a gap in the two-way flow of vehicles. At last she was able to dart across, nearly slipping on the rain-greased street in her brand-new shoes.

'Mr Truesdale!'

'Eh?' He blinked, and didn't seem to recognise her.

'Mr Truesdale, you must come back to the health centre! How long is it since you emptied your bladder?'

'Eh?' he said again, then his vision cleared. 'Oh, golly, not since I got up.'

'And when was that?'

''Bout six. Don't sleep too well, these days…'

'And does it feel full?'

'Eh?' For the third time.

'Your bladder!'

'Bustin'!' he answered frankly. 'I had a big beer an hour ago!'

'Then you really *must* come back!'

Acute urinary retention. Stevie's only experience of the condition was when it had happened to her mother, a distressing but fortunately fleeting symptom of her multiple sclerosis. She had been told then, however, that it could be fatal, leading to kidney failure if not treated promptly.

Fortunately, though, the treatment was simple—passing a catheter through the urethra and into the bladder, which could be done in a doctor's office.

Mr Truesdale was coming with her, reluctant but clearly suffering now, too, from the discomfort of his grossly distended bladder. Entering the waiting room, she saw that Dr Marr had appeared from his office and was about to call his next patient. Going up to him, she quickly forestalled this.

'Dr Marr, you'd better see this patient next.'

Over his shoulder, she saw that Ros Reynolds had overheard her words and was frowning. 'We're not triage nurses,' the centre's manager had said just ten minutes ago.

Julius Marr said quietly, 'What's the problem, Stevie?'

'He can't void his bladder. Mum had the same complaint a couple of years ago, before you started here, and I know it can be dangerous.'

'Yes. Very,' he agreed, then turned to the elderly man. 'Come on, sir, let's get this dealt with immediately.'

They both disappeared into his office, and a minute late she heard him calling for Aimee Hilliard, one of the health centre's nurses, to bring him a catheter pack.

'What was all that about?' Ros asked, curious and still a little sceptical. 'I thought you said you'd only done one year of nursing, fifteen years ago.'

'I have,' Stevie answered, 'but I also had a lot of experience with assorted problems of my mother's, and fortunately this happened to be one of them.'

'I'm glad you had the courage to stick your neck out, then, because I'd probably just have let him go.'

'Thanks, Ros. I must confess, I feel it's the first time today I've been really useful,' she admitted.

'Nonsense,' said the other woman briefly. 'You've coped far better than most for your first day.'

'Is that true? Then thanks again!'

Things settled down again, then at just after six Mr Truesdale emerged, clutching some pamphlets and a prescription form, and approached the reception desk.

'I need to make another appointment,' he said, and Stevie spent the next few minutes patiently helping him to select a day and time.

The waiting room was beginning to empty now. On Wednesdays their last official appointment was at ten to five, but on Tuesdays and Thursdays they stayed open until nine with appointments, and as late as nine-thirty with special clinics, information nights or groups.

Ros began to instruct Stevie in the routine of winding up for the day and she was half-conscious, inwardly, of a sense of pleasant anticipation at the prospect of seeing Dr Marr when he emerged from his office for the last time. He had been so wonderfully supportive at lunch, and she knew she'd earned his good opinion again over the past half hour, with the way she'd insisted that Mr Truesdale return to be seen.

As yet, though, she did not have the slightest inkling that what she felt was dangerous...

She *should* have done, perhaps, because when Ros said she was free to leave she found that she was in no hurry to do so, and stalled for time with a drink of water in the health centre kitchen.

He still hadn't come out, though, and she was being foolish, Stevie realised. Do I really need to see him just so I can hear him tell me I've done well? No, of course I don't!

Firmly, therefore, she gathered her things, said goodbye to those of the office, nursing and medical staff who were in evidence and let herself out the back to where her small two-door car was parked. It was only as she closed the door behind her that she realised Julius—only he hadn't asked her to call him that yet—was hard on her heels.

'Is he going to be all right?' she asked him.

'Hmm?'

'Stan Truesdale.'

'Right.' He summarised with evident impatience. 'He has an enlarged prostate but it doesn't seem too serious. I'll follow it up, of course. I have a patient in the terminal stages of prostate cancer at the moment because he didn't seek treatment until it was too late.'

'And if the problem with—'

She stopped. He hadn't even heard.

Turning away, he flung over his shoulder an utterly absent-minded, 'See you tomorrow, Stevie.' Then he began to stride towards his car. The large briefcase he carried looked heavy and banged against his long legs as he walked.

Frozen with foolish disappointment, Stevie watched him.

He had his car keys at the ready and was opening the driver's door of his dark red Saab as if with another second's delay it might decide to drive off without him.

Then, before she could draw two rather tight-throated breaths, he had flung his briefcase onto the seat behind him, put on his safety belt, wound the window down halfway to let in a rain-cooled breeze, started his engine and reached for the car phone.

Evidently, he didn't even have to dial the number he needed, just pressed a key that automatically reproduced the last number dialled, and spoke seconds later. Walking on woolly legs to her own car, and knowing he was totally oblivious to her presence, Stevie overheard his voice as he manoeuvred the Saab out of its privileged parking space.

'Irene? Hi! I'm on my way now...'

His voice faded as Stevie moved on, and a few seconds later he swept past her, sending up a thick spray of dirty water. She had to jump back to avoid getting her pale linen trousers splashed with grey-brown droplets. Again, he didn't notice, which was...

She hesitated before choosing the word, then accepted reluctantly that it fitted. Inconsiderate. The car park wasn't that narrow. He could have given her a wider berth. He could have avoided that filthy puddle.

He had been inconsiderate to the point of insult, and it jibed so ill with his thoughtful dealings with her over lunch that she almost wondered if that had all been an act.

That's idiotic! she decided. That doesn't make sense at all!

She got out her own car keys, feeling disappointed and confused.

In his car on Anzac Parade, dealing with peak-hour traffic, Julius struggled far harder to switch gears in his mind than he had to struggle with the gears of his engine.

'You have the children with you now?' he said to Irene on the phone, then listened as she proposed a timetable for the rest of the day. 'OK, yes, I'll take them out for pizza, if that will give you a chance to—' He broke off as the light changed and another car made an abrupt change of lane directly in front of him. 'Look, let's talk about it when I get there,' he said. 'I hate talking on the phone while I'm driving. It's not legal, and the traffic's hell... Yes, bye, then.'

He just had time to put the phone back in its cradle when the obsessive lane-changer slammed on his brakes and nearly had the Saab's front bumper halfway into his boot for his reward. Julius shoved the heel of his hand on the hooter—the sort of useless venting of spleen he normally despised—then tried to remind himself that taking an eight-year-old boy and a ten year old girl out for pizza would quite possibly be fun.

Belatedly, he wondered what had happened to Stevie Reid back in the health centre carpark. He had a vague recollection that she'd asked him about Stan Truesdale, and that he had summarised a reply. He might even have managed to say goodbye to her, but beyond that... He shook his head vigorously, fighting the balls of tension growing in the muscles of his temples. He'd be lucky to get home by midnight...

'It *was* his birthday.'

'Sorry?' Stevie looked around, startled, from the huge bank of files she was standing in front of, pulling out those belonging to this morning's scheduled patients. Dr Marr stood there, tall and gorgeously dressed. She'd never known a man who had such a lovely collection of shirts.

Today's was silk, she was sure, in a subtle pattern on a dark background, and she almost reached out to touch it to see just how soft it felt.

She didn't, of course.

He had his glasses in his hand and put them on, in the apparent belief that this would clarify the issue. It didn't, because she was still too busy reacting to his mere presence to connect his words with yesterday's elderly patient. He explained finally. 'Stan Truesdale. It *was* his birthday yesterday.'

'Oh, it was? He put down March the tenth, I noticed, but I thought he might just have been confused about what he was supposed to write.'

'That was probably the more likely possibility,' Dr Marr conceded, 'but, no, I checked and that's what he said. He was pleased because his daughter in Melbourne had sent a card and promised to come up soon.'

'I'm glad he has a daughter. I had the impression he wasn't looking after himself very well.'

'No. His wife died last year, apparently...and so did the doctor they'd been going to for years, which was why we hadn't seen him before, and why he'd delayed seeking attention for too long. I'm going to put him in touch with the community nursing service because I think he needs a little more help than he's going to look for on his own. They may assess the need for further assistance after a home visit, too.'

'Good,' Stevie agreed. 'I'm glad of that. I won't enjoy seeing patients who aren't coping in other aspects of their lives.'

'It's part of medicine, Stevie,' he pointed out soberly. 'The social safety net in this country does have some holes, although it's better than in many places. I think a health centre like this is a good place to catch people like Stan

Truesdale before he falls through one of those holes, and I tell the office staff to let the medical staff know if there's anything they think we haven't picked up on. Any clues from their behaviour in the waiting room, or questions they ask you. That goes for you, too, obviously, with any patient.'

'I'll remember that.'

'But listen…' He changed tack suddenly. 'I have to apologise. I think I cut you off in the car park yesterday.'

'No, you didn't quite cut me off, but I almost got my clothes splashed,' she answered lightly. What a relief to find he at least had the grace to apologise! But now she received only a blank look.

'I meant when we were talking,' he said. 'I'm afraid I was lost in thought.'

'Right. Of course. No, it was fine.' She put on a smile and lifted her chin. 'I could tell you were…' She hesitated. A million miles away? 'Tired.'

'But…' he frowned '…what was that about? Your clothes?'

'Nothing,' she insisted quickly, while thinking, He still doesn't have a clue that I was even there. What's on his mind that it can absorb him so? He hasn't struck me as the kind of man who makes a habit of it. 'I thought you meant something else.'

And before he could probe further and get the somewhat embarrassing truth from her that *he* was so absent-minded and *she* so totally insignificant that he'd come within a foot of sideswiping her trousers with his wet, dirty wheels and hadn't even seen her, she turned with an emphatic performance of concentration to her wall of files.

CHAPTER THREE

IT TOOK Stevie a scant two weeks to realise that, on the subject of Julius Marr, she was seriously in trouble. The full truth of it came to her in a familiar way—she started to write songs.

An only child, Stevie had been wrapped up in music all her life—piano-playing until she was twelve, folk guitar and school choir in her teens, and some abortive and, in retrospect, hilarious attempts after leaving school to make a career of it.

She had done waitressing while having voice lessons, played solo folk guitar in a pub and actually formed a heavy metal rock band with a schoolfriend, Alex, and her two wild-haired and studiously thug-like brothers.

But Swamp Thing had broken up before playing its first gig, and the brothers, David and Paul, were now very conservative businessmen with plush offices in a glass-skinned high-rise in North Sydney.

Then, at twenty-three, Stevie had realised she wanted to do much more with her life than struggle on the fringes of a singing career. First she'd started nursing and then she'd met Grant Hall, had fallen in love and got engaged.

This latter event meant that her musical life had consisted for nearly a year of writing awful songs in which 'true love' inevitably rhymed with 'sky above' or, even worse, 'turtle dove'. What *was* a turtle dove, anyway? And the treacly chorus got repeated at least six times.

It also meant that she'd given up nursing after only a year.

'I'm sorry, Stephanie,' Grant said, 'But nursing just isn't a career that works for a corporate wife, as you're going to be. I expect I'll be sent overseas for several years soon— probably Hong Kong—and I'll need a wife with social and entertaining skills, not one who can get a four-year-old to take an injection without crying. If you're serious about our marriage, and my career, you'll give up nursing after your exams and do some courses in cordon bleu cooking and good grooming.'

Still starry-eyed with new love, Stevie conceded his point and embarked on her cordon bleu course. She became, and still was, an excellent cook, but it wasn't an easy decision, and she had to swallow a lot of regret. She also baulked at the good grooming! At the time, though, the choice she made, at the end of the day, seemed obvious, sensible, right.

But their engagement didn't last. Mum wasn't well, and after what seemed like an endless battery of tests, a diagnosis was made—multiple sclerosis. Having lost her father when she was sixteen to heart failure, Stevie was devastated and terrified. She didn't entertain for a moment the possibility of putting Mum in a nursing home once the disease took hold, and told Grant so straight out.

She expected, of course, that he would understand and support this, as she understood and supported his career goals, but shockingly he didn't, and once again she was forced to choose.

This time, the choice itself was not painful or difficult. She would nurse Mum and Grant could have his ring back right now! But her discovery that Grant only paid lip service to the sentiments she wrote about so naïvely in her songs hurt badly and threatened for a while to embitter her. Her songs, at that point, tended to feature relentless rhymes of the bleak/weak or lonely death/wintry breath variety.

Then, when she was thirty-one and working part time for

a charity, while Mum got worse in typically irregular patterns of good and bad periods, Alex, now married with a baby, rang up out of the blue to say that she'd discovered country music, she was forming an all-women band, and she wanted Stevie to sing lead vocals.

'I can't,' Stevie insisted, until her mother made her change her mind.

'If nothing else,' she said with a laugh, 'because I'd adore to do all your outfits!'

Thus was born Lizzy in the Kitchen, and they played together with just a couple of changes of line-up for nearly eight years.

The band made several positive changes in Stevie's life. Most important, perhaps, it gave her an outlet for her emotions, her energy and her creativity. It taught her, as she got to know the husbands of the other band members, that not all men were like Grant.

And it gave her the chance to write some much better songs. She didn't rhyme 'you' with 'true' for ten years.

Until, taking a restless, barefoot walk along Maroubra beach after work on the second Tuesday of her employment at the Southshore Health Centre, she suddenly found herself humming a new tune and fitting snatched phrases to it as images of Julius Marr, which were so real she could almost reach out and touch them, filled her mind.

'Walking with you, I'd always be true…' she sang under her breath as autumn waves curled and foamed onto the shore and patient surfers bobbed like seals out in the blue-green swell, waiting for their moment. 'Oh, *yuck*! Did I really sing that? What's the matter with me?'

Three minutes of close analysis brought enlightenment.

'It's Dr Marr. Dr Marr…Julius.'

It felt heavenly just to say his name and, having never given more than a passing thought to that particular combination of syllables, she suddenly decided it was one of the most beautiful—and also, perhaps fortunately, most un-rhymable—male names in the English language.

The whole thing felt wonderful at first. Just to know there was someone like him in the world…in her life…and that she could see him almost every day. To realise that she was coming to know the full repertoire of his lovely shirts, the way he liked his coffee, the sound of his laugh and the rhythm of his feet in the corridors of the health centre.

To feel the tender new bud of her physical attraction to him begin to swell and unfurl. God, how long had it been since she'd felt *that* for a man? That quickening of the pulses, that weakness in her legs, that butterfly feeling in her stomach.

Yes, how long *had* it been? Apart from the most fleeting attractions to a handful of men whose lives had brushed against hers only in the briefest and lightest of ways, Stevie had known nothing like this since her engagement to Grant, and that had been fourteen years ago.

I'm thirty-nine. This is the way teenagers feel. They love it. They thrive on rushing from cloud nine to the pit of despair and back again in the space of an hour over a hunky male, but *me…now…* It didn't feel wonderful any more. It felt terrifying.

Terrifying or not, however, it was a heady cocktail. She left the beach and drove home, oblivious to the beauty of the sunset that had begun to unfold overhead. She made scrambled eggs on toast for dinner, and then couldn't finish them because suddenly food was too mundane and unim-portant to bother with. She was feasting on the magical nourishment of passion.

Stevie slept badly that night because her mind was too full of images of Julius—the cheerful way he greeted his regular patients, the wide smile that could be expressive of wry, complex emotions as well as simple pleasure, and even the times when he swept through the waiting room of the health centre and didn't seem to see anyone at all.

And it was a dangerous sign that she found even *this* endearing, because to the rest of the staff it could be distinctly irritating.

'Oh, Dr Marr, I was wondering if you had time to sign—'

Bang! Ros's unfinished sentence on a Friday afternoon after Stevie's third restless night in a row was punctuated by the sound of Julius's office door being closed carelessly behind him.

Ros shrugged at Stephanie. 'I think he's getting worse!'

'Has he always been like this, then?' Another unmistakable symptom, this—desperately wanting to learn more about him, and having to pretend that her question was only casually curious.

'He's only been here since last January,' Ros answered. 'He started about three weeks before I came here from a group practice of obstetricians, so we were both finding our feet together. He was extremely keen to get to grips with the routine of the centre, which he did, very quickly. His rapport with patients is always very good—well, you'd have known that before you started here—but lately, when he isn't actually seeing people, he's seemed so preoccupied. I've been wondering if he's having personal problems.'

'He's married, of course,' Stevie said now, her mouth dry. Heaven help her, she was far gone enough to have looked closely at his left hand on Wednesday in case there was a ring. There wasn't, but not all married men wore them.

Now, just tell me he's blissfully married, Ros, and I'll get this under control. I really must, because that song I spent two hours on last night was appalling when I reread it this morning!

'To be honest,' Ros was saying thoughtfully, 'I'm not absolutely sure.'

'Right...'

'I'd say he isn't because he's never mentioned a wife or children but, then, perhaps he wouldn't because he doesn't tend to talk much about his private life. Lately, as I said, he's been rushing off with that big black frown on his face the moment he finishes here, but I don't know what he's rushing *to*. There is a woman who rings him here fairly often, though, come to think of it... Irene. If you really want to know, I could look up his personnel file and see what he's put for marital status and next of kin.'

'No,' said Stevie lightly. 'It's not important. And it's not our business, is it, if it's something he doesn't choose to talk about openly?'

She wished profoundly that Ros had given a more definite answer, because now the door to her foolish hopes was wide open. Commendably incurious, the centre manager had now disappeared into her own office, leaving Stevie to reassert her good sense on this whole lamentable subject.

There was really only one reason why successful, intelligent, physically commanding men of Julius Marr's age were single—because they wanted to be. If they *didn't* want to be, then it was very obvious that they were dating. Therefore he either was married, and perhaps the female caller—Irene—was his wife, or he was contentedly wedded to his work and his hobbies.

Stevie was a woman with her feet on the ground, and it didn't take her long to realise where the true problem lay.

I'm lonely. I put the idea of love aside after my disillusionment over Grant, and while I was caring for Mum all those years. Now Mum is gone and my days are fuller, my world has got bigger and I'm ready for more. I'd like to meet a man. I'd like to go out, to really fall in love, to get serious about someone, to get married...

Lizzy in the Kitchen was playing twice this weekend, once at Liz's son's school fête on Saturday morning and once at a wedding late on Saturday afternoon. The latter was a large, loud, sprawling outdoor event, with the groom dressed as a cowboy and the bride, in bright pink, looking like an extra in a John Wayne movie—a female saloon-keeper of doubtful morals, perhaps.

This was not the sort of wedding that Stevie had aspired to for herself during her engagement to Grant, but she found herself painfully envious of the billowing bride none-theless. She even said so to Alex before she could stop herself, as they packed away the band's equipment after a rousing and well-received set of twelve songs.

'What, in *that* dress?' Alex returned in a drawl.

'No, not in that dress! But, Alex, I'd like to get married, and I'm afraid I've left it too late. It just didn't seem pos-sible when Mum was alive. For a long time I didn't want to, then I didn't meet anyone and didn't really think about it. Now... And it's probably too late,' she repeated.

'Nonsense,' answered Alex briskly as she put her electric violin into its case.

'But I mean...'

'No, it's nonsense,' her friend insisted. 'There are plenty of men out there—'

'Says the woman who hasn't looked at one since Nick came along.'

'And you're an attractive, interesting and financially se-cure woman, still of child-bearing age.'

'Just. Possibly. You do come to the point, don't you?'

'It's what people like about me,' Alex pointed out truthfully, then added with a grin and an equal degree of truth, 'Except for the people that *don't*!'

'What men, though, Alex?' Stevie persisted.

'Liz's husband?' Ex-husband, she meant, but Stevie was aghast all the same.

'*Pete?*'

'Why not? He's nice. Their divorce was about as amicable as you can get without staying married. And the kids are nice.'

'I suppose perhaps that's it,' Stevie confessed. 'The kids. They're almost grown up, at fourteen and seventeen. I'm not convinced I'd make a good stepmother, and I very much doubt Pete would want to start again with another baby. And anyway—' She broke off with a bemused laugh. 'This is ridiculous! As nice as he is, I don't find...' Liz herself walked past at that moment, wheeling her drum kit on a trolley. Stevie lowered her voice. 'I don't find Pete remotely attractive.'

'Well, if there's no one you already *know*,' Alex said, stretching her tall body to scan the crowd of wedding guests as if a suitable male might emerge from their ranks at that very moment, 'Then you must take action to find one.'

'Take action,' Stevie echoed sceptically. 'How?'

'Tell your friends to fix you up.'

'No, thanks!'

'Do a course in oxyacetylene welding.'

'You're joking!'

'Start taking your washing to a laundromat.'

'*Why?*'

'Well-known fact. Single men frequent laundromats. You can tell a lot about someone from the state of their undergar—'

'Alex...!'

'I mean it, woman! If something's important to you, you

can't just sit around and wait for it to happen. You have to go out and get it.'

The words stuck in Stevie's mind and she knew they were true. How many people, for example, had said to her over the years, 'I wish I could sing or play an instrument'? And then they never took the first step of phoning a teacher to find out about lessons.

By the end of the weekend, Stevie had made a decision. She wasn't going to think about Julius any more. That was foolish and unproductive. And she wasn't going to wallow in 'if only…' She was going to take action, as Alex had advised. And she knew what action she was going to take, too.

She was going to advertise.

There was a very nice, glossy lifestyle magazine in the newsagent every week called *Sydney Scene* and it featured at least two pages of 'personal' ads in each issue. Stevie's appeared in the second week of April, when the mornings had started to chill down a little, the days were beginning to close in and there was a new, zesty freshness in the air.

Autumn. Traditionally a time of mellow nostalgia, not of new, spring-like beginnings. But Stevie was not the sort of woman to knuckle under to a cliché.

The wording of her advertisement was simple and, she hoped, accurate rather than pretentious. 'Female, 39, intelligent, cultured, creative, sincere and secure, seeks male for friendship/partnership.'

It was nestled halfway down a column of ads whose authors frequently made much bolder claims. 'Zany, gorgeous brunette' and 'stunningly successful blonde' were two of them. Nonetheless, Stevie received a good clutch of responses, via the private mail-box at the magazine, which guaranteed security and privacy.

She spent a whole evening reading the letters and deciding which ones she would ring first. She then chatted—nervously—on the phone to three men and made arrangements to meet each of them after work next week, on Monday, Tuesday and Wednesday, in a busy bar-restaurant called Bravos down the road from the health centre, just off Anzac Parade.

She planned to catch a taxi home each time because she was aware that she was potentially vulnerable. None of these men would find out her last name, where she lived and worked or the make and registration of the car she drove until she was quite sure that they were what they seemed.

She caught the bus to work on Monday and hoped she wouldn't be nervous about her five forty-five rendezvous all day. This turned out not to be a problem, as the centre was far too busy. Poor Sally Kitchin, who'd already been in last week for her triplets' two-month immunisation, was here again, with all three of them crying at once.

Dr Marr was running late and they were all hungry for a feed. She could manage two of them at once, but the third needed a supplementary bottle and Stevie finally offered to prepare and give it herself, as she was mainly handling the appointment line today and often had some time between calls.

'But don't heat it in the microwave,' Sally warned anxiously. She had to be propelled by some encouraging words towards the tiny room where she would be able to feed the other two in private.

'Why not?' Stevie asked blankly, feeling inadequate. She had little Amelia up on her shoulder and the poor mite was still crying.

Sally looked at her, horrified. 'You just mustn't. I've read it. You mustn't heat bottles in the microwave. It—it curdles the milk, I suppose.'

'Really?' Stevie couldn't help betraying a little scepticism, although from Sally's face it was as inflexible a rule as the one about not giving babies plastic bags to play with, and the danger involved was apparently every bit as acute.

Stevie frowned, holding baby and sterilised bottle in one hand and Sally's tin of powdered soya formula in the other.

Dr Marr came past to call his next patient. Not the triplets' turn yet, unfortunately. 'What's the problem?' he said cheerfully.

'Nothing. Everything's fine,' Sally assured him quickly.

But Stevie said, 'Why isn't it safe to heat bottles in the microwave? Sally's been told that it isn't, but isn't sure why.'

'Well, only because it's so much easier to be careless about temperature that way. A microwave heats unevenly, and it doesn't heat the bottle itself. That only gets hots once the warmed milk has had a chance to heat it. So if you're in a rush you can feel the cool bottle and toss a tepid drop of milk onto your wrist and think, That feels fine. In fact, some of the milk might be scalding hot and burn the baby's mouth. As long as you shake it thoroughly and then wait a few moments before you test it, it should be fine.'

'Good,' Stevie said firmly, above the protesting Amelia. 'I'll do it that way, then.'

Sally gave a suspicious look back at Stevie and the baby as if she might veto the plan at the last moment, then reluctantly moved forward into the little treatment room while Stevie dashed back to answer the phone, then escaped its demands for long enough to heat the bottle.

In view of Sally's scepticism, she was then over-cautious about the possibility of heating the formula too much and had to give it several bursts in the microwave because she'd only chosen a few seconds on the electronic timer each time.

'It will be ready eventually,' she promised Amelia, who was as frantic as a baby bird now. 'Hopefully before you're old enough to start school!'

And then, finally, it was, and the little girl nestled happily into her arms, closed her eyes and began to suck blissfully. It gave Stevie a lovely feeling—even when she had to get the phone again and juggle phone, pen, baby and bottle in two inexperienced hands.

It made her wonder about tonight and her rendezvous at Bravos. Was it really possible to meet a man that way? Could someone start out as a stranger and end up, a year or two down the track, as the father of her baby? A baby just like this…

Well, of course! Short of being childhood sweethearts, people had to meet for the first time at some point, and they met in all sorts of ways. Why not like this?

Distracted, she didn't notice Dr Marr's approach until he said, 'I'm ready for them now, if you are.'

'Oh. Fine. Sorry. Um, she hasn't quite finished. Shall I…?'

She was absurdly flustered and prepared to hand the baby to him then and there, the bottle still in its mouth, but he forestalled her with a gentle push that snuggled the baby back into her arms.

'Would you mind?' he said. 'Ros and Cathy can take the phones. Aimee's doing a dressing for Dr Williams. Could you help Sally manage them while I take a look at each? See how she's pulling her ear? I suspect they have ear infections…'

They did, and Dr Marr did a thorough and wonderful job of explaining why, how ear infections should be treated and what could be done to minimise their occurrence. Sally took in every word with a strained expression on her face, as if she were to be tested on the information for an exam first thing next morning.

During his explanation Dr Marr looked at Stevie, who was still holding Amelia, almost as often as he looked at Sally, and she wanted to say to him, Don't! I have no use for this information. I'm not a mother. I probably never will be.

When Sally left with her babies—only one crying now—and her prescription, her huge perambulator and bursting nappy bag, Stevie suddenly found that the day had gone flat and she couldn't look forward to meeting a strange man tonight.

Perhaps it wasn't surprising, then, that the hour she spent with him over drinks wasn't very successful. Stuart seemed like a perfectly presentable person, a futures analyst—whatever that entailed—at the stock exchange. Tall and quite nice-looking. Divorced with no children. Aged forty… although Stevie did privately wonder if he'd shaved a few years off his real age with that figure. He definitely looked older than Julius…

Somehow, they completely and utterly failed to click and, though both were polite enough to avoid mentioning the fact, they parted without him asking for her phone number, and Stevie knew that they would not see each other again.

Tuesday evening was a repeat performance. Chris was 'in advertising', aged thirty-five, never married, very smooth, perfectly amiable. He asked for Stevie's phone number out of tact and nothing else, and would almost certainly never dial it.

Arriving home by taxi to eat leftover tuna casserole at six fifty-five, Stevie almost phoned Wednesday's man—'call me John'—to cancel.

But that's cowardly, she decided. My goodness, if I remotely expect anything to come of it, I have to persevere for longer than this!

Newly resolved, she dressed with extra care the next morning in a brand-new skirt of finely woven wool plaid and a short-sleeved black Angora knit top, and made her fresh make-up almost glamorous in the bathroom at the health centre after work.

Feeling like a veteran as she went through the front door of Bravos and turned left towards the elegant bar, she reflected that this was emerging as the moment she really hated. That first encounter, when you weren't absolutely sure that you were making eye contact with the right man, and when you knew that, for every telling first impression you were getting of *him*, he was getting the same of *you*.

Steeling herself for it, trying to conjure out of the few facts she had gleaned from their rather brief phone conversation last week what 'call me John' might look like, Stevie entered the bar.

Today, though, something was different, and Stevie was hit by the appalled realisation that, in all her careful planning against making herself vulnerable to a stranger, she had overlooked one vital consideration. This place was far too close to the health centre, and a far more likely danger lay in the possibility that someone she knew would be here too.

That danger was now a reality. Standing at the bar and glancing at his watch, there stood Julius Marr.

He hadn't seen her yet. She stopped, washed by the heat of her dismay. For about ten seconds she entertained the absurd notion that Dr Marr himself was 'call me John'. Unlike Stuart and Chris, this third man, who had signed his letter merely, 'Your new friend', had sounded distinctly cagey on the phone.

Stevie had put it down to nerves, but it was entirely possible that there was a more sinister explanation. 'Call me John' was married, and in search of a discreet affair on the side.

But 'call me John' could not possibly be Julius Marr. She'd been completely honest, herself, on the phone—had said her name was Stephanie, shortened to Stevie, had said she was a medical receptionist. The voice hadn't been familiar. And he never would have arranged a meeting, knowing it was her. Besides, he wasn't the type, surely, to engage in such double deceit?

In the time it had taken all this to run through her mind, however, Julius had turned to scan the restaurant foyer and had seen her, which meant she could only go forward to greet him with a casual smile on her face.

'Meeting someone?' he said.

'Yes. Are you?'

'Hope so.' He frowned and looked at his watch again. 'She's late.'

'So's mine.'

'Shall we have a drink together, then, while we wait?'

'That'd be nice,' she answered at once, then rethought the matter and blurted aloud, 'Only, if I'm sitting with you, he won't realise I'm the person he's come to meet. He'll be looking for someone sitting alone.'

'But surely…' He frowned, and Stevie crumbled inside as he demanded, puzzled, 'Doesn't this man know what you look—?'

'It's a blind date,' she confessed hastily, hiding her miserable embarrassment. 'He knows nothing about me at all.'

'In that case,' he agreed gravely, betraying not a hint of amusement or disapproval, 'Perhaps you're right. You'd better sit by yourself. I wouldn't want to spoil your evening.'

'No...' Although, heaven help me, I'd far rather spend it with you...

'You look lovely, by the way.' There was a new light in his eyes now, but Stevie was still too flustered to wonder what it signified. 'I meant to tell you so earlier in the day but I didn't get the chance.'

'Thank you.'

She moved to one of the small tables and angled her chair at the precise point where he could not have considered that she had her back to him but where she could see him only as a blur in the corner of her eye nonetheless.

A minute later, a large gin and tonic arrived, brought by a black-garbed young waiter with the message, 'With the compliments of the gentleman at the bar.'

Stevie managed a half-smile at Dr Marr as he raised his glass to her. Then she waited. And waited. And waited. As did he.

Finally, he came over to her, holding his almost empty glass. 'It seems we've both been stood up,' he said, with the wicked hint of a smile.

'It does look that way,' she agreed, feeling relief more than anything else.

He sat down, and set down his drink. 'It's his loss, of course. But you were hoping for an evening out with an interesting man. Could you possibly consider me as a substitute?'

Looking up to meet his slate-eyed gaze, she answered, 'Thank you, Dr Marr. That would be lovely.'

'Only,' he said with a sudden hint of steel in his voice, 'if you call me Dr Marr one more time, I'll send for the bill then and there! Make it Julius, please, as Ros and everyone else does, except when there are patients to overhear.'

'Julius.' She said it aloud to him for the first time and saw him watching her mouth as the sounds came.

Their evening was magical, and his gallantry flawless. Not once did he refer to the unnamed woman who had failed to meet him here as planned, and not once did he refer to Stevie's own fickle unknown, who'd evidently had second thoughts about his venture into infidelity.

The way he's treating me, this could have been something we'd planned with each other days ago, Stevie thought with hazy, dangerous happiness. It was against her nature to do things by halves. At this precise moment, the rest of the world barely existed at all.

On Monday and Tuesday, with Stuart and Chris, she had not intended to eat here at Bravos, even if the drinks hour had gone wonderfully well. The restaurant part of the establishment was elegant and expensive and she did not want to set up any suspicion that she was playing along for the sake of a cushy night out at her companion's expense. If dinner had been suggested by either man, she would have proposed a more modest Italian eatery down the road.

Julius, though, waved this suggestion aside imperiously. 'It's a cool evening and there was rain forecast. Why not just stay here? The food is very good.'

It would have been tasteless of her to protest, so she settled down to enjoy the dry white wine, stuffed mushrooms, Caesar salad and fettuccine with scampi in a cream sauce, ending with coffee and chocolate-hazelnut torte.

The food, though, came a distant second to the company. If she had liked Julius as her mother's doctor, and had developed a definite crush on him as her professional colleague, she started to fall seriously in love with him that night as they talked and as she learned more about him.

'Where were you before coming to Southshore?' she asked him as they ate.

She expected to hear that he'd been at another health centre, or perhaps in practice on his own somewhere, but to her surprise he answered, 'In the accident and emergency department at Southshore Hospital, brushing up on my practical skills for a year. For twelve years before that, I was in medical research at Sydney University, and never encountered patients at all, except as lines of computer data and statistics on a graph.'

'That's quite a change to make, from the rarefied atmosphere of research to a busy health centre like ours.'

'Ours?' he echoed, his wide mouth curving. 'You're starting to get a bit possessive about the place, then?'

'Yes, I love it, now that I'm relaxed enough to handle the pace.'

'I'm glad. And, yes, it was quite a change. Deliberately so.'

'Why?'

'I found I didn't like the person I'd become,' he said seriously. 'Totally wrapped up in my work, forgetting to what extent medicine—all medicine, even the driest research—is about people, having very little life at all outside my lab and my office at the university. The people who cared about me got short shrift and scant attention, and that's a loss that can never be made up. I even thought for a long time that I—' He broke off abruptly and shook his head.

'That you…?' she prompted gently, but again came that negative movement of his head.

'No. I don't want to get into all that. It's over now, and the changes I've made I haven't regretted one bit. There's a lot I can now see clearly about my life back then that I couldn't see at all at the time.'

'And you have no contact at all with the research scene now?'

He hesitated for a moment and then answered, 'Some. A little. More than I'd like sometimes!' His wry smile was heavily nuanced. 'I'm still working all that out. Things should be more settled in a few months' time. Forgive me, but if I sometimes seem preoccupied at work that's the reason.'

'Why don't you talk about it, then?' she ventured, thinking of Ros Reynolds's conjectures on the subject.

'Because it's my problem. Please, don't talk at work about the things we say to each other tonight.' He met her gaze openly, seeking for her assent, and she gave it with a nod.

'Of course I won't.'

'You see, it's unfair to subject— Well, let's just say there are…people I have the power to hurt, and I don't want to risk doing that by saying more than I should to anyone who isn't involved.'

The arrival of more coffee punctuated this statement, and he accepted another cup as if relieved to be able to close the subject. Stevie was quite happy about that, and quite happy to accept his words at face value.

They made sense, and when he asked her in a teasing sort of way how Lizzy was going in her kitchen she told him about the cowboy wedding of three Saturdays ago, being just a little witty and unkind about the vast, saddle-shaped cake and the twelve bridesmaids dressed in Annie Oakley outfits.

'It must have been quite an occasion!' he said.

'It was! And, I must say, everyone had a fabulous time, judging by the amount of noise and dancing. We had to do two encores and my voice was giving out.'

'How on earth did you come by your name?' he wanted to know.

'Courtesy of Liz's ex-husband, though he didn't know

how creative he was being. We were practising at their house—they were still married, then—in the very early days when we couldn't *possibly* have played in public, and he came into the room and said, 'Do you know what you lot sound like? Lizzy in the kitchen, singing while she cooks, clattering the pots and pans.' First I wrote a song with those lines in it. Did you hear how well they scan? Then we thought the first bit would make a great name for the band.'

'I agree. Clever Pete.'

'Hey! Hang on!' she pointed out indignantly. 'He just *said* it! *We* were the ones who realised it had possibilities!'

They both laughed, then he said much more seriously, 'It must have made a big difference to your mum, knowing you had that in your life.'

'Oh, it did,' she agreed. 'She was quite able to be left alone for the time it took to do a gig, as long as I set her up properly beforehand and got a neighbour to look in for five minutes if I was going to be gone extra long. And we usually practised at my place so I didn't have to leave her for that. She loved listening to us.'

'I can imagine.'

'And she was much happier about me looking after her at home because she knew I was fulfilled in other ways.'

'And was it enough, Stevie?' he asked in his low, burred voice. 'I have wondered about that since I've known you. Is it enough now?'

She stared down into her coffee and swirled it absently.

'Not quite, no,' she admitted quietly. 'Particularly now that she's gone. No, Lizzy in the Kitchen isn't quite enough any more.'

He captured her restless hand and covered it with his on the table, then caressed it with his forefinger, running it across her knuckles and tracing the blue lines of the veins that ran visibly beneath her fine skin. 'Something else I've been wondering just lately... Would you let me try to fill the gap, Stevie?' he asked.

CHAPTER FOUR

STEVIE didn't need to give Julius an answer. It was there in her face as she looked up at him. He leaned across the table and brushed his lips against hers. Just the briefest of kisses...or so Stevie thought until he made a little sound of need in his throat and came back for more.

This time she was more than ready for him and lifted her face towards his as she parted her lips. He tasted exquisitely of coffee and chocolate and wine, and her whole body was sizzling with the magic of the touch of his mouth.

He brushed his cheek along her jaw and she felt the male roughness of it, caught the faint, woody scent of his aftershave, and felt the feather soft prickle of his eyelashes as he tilted his head across the other way to taste her differently. Then, too soon, very slowly, he pulled fractionally away.

'Not here,' he whispered against her. 'Let's go...'

She could only nod mutely, overcome by the suddenness of it, the wonderfulness of it, the impossibility of it.

I was so sure it was just a foolish crush, she thought. And now, to find that he feels it too!

No questions or doubts entered her mind at that moment. There was no room. Every bit of her seemed full of him—his voice in her ears, his taste on her tongue, his warm, masculine scent in her nostrils mingling with the savoury aromas of food as they left the restaurant with arms twisted together and hands clasped. Her legs were shaking, and she could have clung to him for ever.

Outside, he asked, 'Have you got your car?'

'No. I was going to take a taxi.'

'Good. Then we can go together.'

'Where, Julius?' Her voice came out husky, and the question was so provocative that she would have bitten it back if she could.

But there was no hesitation before his answer.

'To your place. Is that all right? May I come in, to be alone with you for a while? It's not late, Stevie. I'd love to be with you for a few hours more tonight...' His hand splayed out over the curve of her hip and she could feel its heat, although the gesture was light, demanding nothing.

Scarcely even troubling to hide her bliss, she said yes to his question.

When he touched her again, as soon as they'd entered the darkened house, she was still trembling, and when she tried to reach out a hand to switch on the light in the front hallway he coaxed her arm downwards.

'No, no...' he said. 'Darkness is nice. Let me kiss you in the dark, Stevie...'

He did, and if it had felt wonderful in the restaurant, it felt ten times better now that they were alone. She was tiny against him, but that didn't seem to matter. He bent down to her and scooped her face against his with his warm hands, drinking the taste of her until she was breathless and her mouth was swollen.

Then he lifted her off the ground with his arms wrapped around her hips, and she gave a delighted gurgle of laughter and bent to him now, combing her fingers through his thick, dark hair, moulding his roughened jaw with her palms, drinking him in.

At last, though, he set her down and she said hazily aloud, 'I should offer you...I don't know...hot cocoa? More wine?'

'Nothing,' he answered. 'Except the chance to sit on that

comfortable couch with you and keep you in my arms for much, much longer.'

So they kissed and talked and kissed again and time drifted past…or they drifted through time, like swans on a river, and it didn't matter that it was eleven, eleven-thirty, midnight…until, caressing his face again and staring into it, she suddenly saw how his eyes glittered with fatigue and his skin was like paper around the corners of his eyes.

'You're exhausted, Julius.'

'I know.' He winced and blinked, then pressed his fingers into his eyes. 'Sorry. Does it show?'

'I'm the one who should apologise. I've been keeping you here…'

'Oh, against my will? Is that what you're saying?'

She laughed. 'Well, no, but…' Then she stopped and took a breath. 'Actually, if you want to, you can…' Stay. Sleep with me.

Something she hadn't asked a man before, ever. She'd slept with Grant after they'd become engaged, but he had been the one to make all the moves while she had put on the brakes for ages. So to say this to Julius, now, when she knew him so little…

Except, she reflected, that wasn't really true. She'd known him for well over a year. He had helped her through Mum's death and dying. He had come to the funeral. He had given her a job, and now, for the past five weeks, she'd been seeing him almost every day.

Still, though, she realised in time that it was too dangerous, and too important. She wasn't ready to say it or to act on it yet and so she stopped. He came in, not having perceived the direction of her unfinished sentence, 'Just tell me, make it easy for me to see you at work tomorrow. When can I see you and be with you like this again?'

'Tomorrow evening?' she said weakly.

There was no point in playing hard to get. He had her at least three-quarters won already and he must know it. His open eagerness was overwhelming and wonderful, too. Emotion like this was something she understood, thrived on, responded to.

His eyes lit up wickedly at her words. 'Now, does that mean Thursday? Or Friday?'

'Thursday.'

'In that case, it's *today*...'

'And is that good?'

'It's great...' He planted a trail of hot kisses all along her collar-bone and up her neck, then nuzzled at the tender weight of her ear lobe. It sent wire-thin lines of electricity radiating all through her. 'Except that I have to work late.'

'So do I,' she recalled. There was a stop-smoking course running from seven-thirty until eight, and late appointment hours as well, until nine, and she would be staffing the front desk and locking up the centre. 'Are you doing the class, or...?'

'No,' he said quickly. 'Not at the health centre. On the computer. I'll do it at home. You're closing the place at nine?'

'Yes.'

'I'll pick you up, then.'

'From there, or here?'

'Which would you prefer, Stevie? It's up to you.' He was watching her closely.

'Home, I think. Here,' she answered. 'I—I don't want—'

'No,' he agreed at once. 'Best not to shout these things from the rooftops.'

Except that's exactly what I'd like to do, Stevie realised. Or, at least, I'm not sure that I'll be able to help myself. Surely it will be obvious to everyone just because of how happy I am!

The rest of the staff at the Southshore Health Centre were evidently pitiably lacking in perception, however, because the stars and rainbows that flashed and undulated around Stevie all the next day were apparently quite invisible to them, as was the fact that her feet didn't quite touch the ground and her soft smile rarely left her face.

Julius noticed, though. It was wonderful to call him Julius, instead of studiously thinking of him as Dr Marr. And Julius looked pretty happy, too…or would have done if he hadn't been too palpably fatigued.

'You didn't go home and work last night after you left my place, did you?' she scolded him softly during a brief moment alone in his office. Neither of them dared to touch the other, but it wasn't hard to know that he wanted to.

'Not for long.'

'Not long is still *too* long when you get home at twelve forty-five and start work at eight-thirty!'

But was that far too possessive and presumptuous and, yes, *wifely* for a new relationship? she wondered afterwards. He hadn't seemed to mind, yet she was aware that it would be so easy for her to care too much about him too soon. She already did.

And surely this tenderness couldn't extend as far as feeling anything for his patients? Somehow, it seemed to…

Stan Truesdale arrived to see Julius shortly after lunch, with a scheduled appointment this time and looking much better than he had done a few weeks ago. His clothes were clean and neat, and he was freshly shaved, with his rather sparse grey hair neatly brushed.

He seemed very satisfied with his appointment, too, and quite happy to share the details with Stevie, whom he evidently remembered in a positive light after the way she'd helped him on that first day.

'He's sending me to a urologist, and he thinks I'll probably have to have it drilled,' he reported to Stevie, who was interested but was trying to make an appointment for another patient and answer the phone at the same time. Mr Truesdale didn't seem to mind that he could be overheard by at least two other people.

'Drilled?' Stevie echoed, rather faintly. Did urologists tackle dental work these days? Of course they didn't! And Mr Truesdale's problem area was his prostate.

'Yes,' he answered her. 'No, I s'pose that's not what it's called. Now, what's it called? That's right. A rebore!' There was quite a satisfied note as he came up with the right word, and he departed very cheerfully.

Stevie couldn't quite share his optimism. Without realising it, she wore a pained and anxious expression, and a moment later she felt the brush of Julius's arm as he reached past her for his next patient's file.

'Mr Truesdale was a plumber before his retirement,' he murmured drily, so close that she could feel his warmth.

'A plumber?'

'Yes, so the idea of a rebore to remove the constriction that his prostate is creating around his urethra makes immediate sense to him. Like unblocking a drainpipe.'

'It's a little…uh…graphic for those of us who don't even have a prostate…'

'It's a very routine operation these days. His urologist will do it in hospital, under epidural anaesthesia, without even needing to open up the lower abdomen. He'll have a few days in hospital afterwards while he's flushed through, and when there's no further sign of bleeding he'll be discharged. It'll take some weeks for him to fully heal internally, but after that he should notice a marked improvement in his flow and control. Feeling better?'

'Yes. Thank you!'

'Good…' He took the file he'd come for and called the

name of his next patient, and she couldn't help watching after him for several seconds longer than she should have done.

There was a small emergency late in the afternoon. Very small. 'About three kilograms, I'd say,' Julius told the expectant first-time mother, opening the examining-room door for her after her appointment.

'Do you take bets?' she asked. 'Because to me it already feels a lot heavier and I'm not due for three more days. If I go late—'

'Mrs Robertson, no doctor in his right mind would take bets on anything connected with childbirth,' he answered, and, as if to prove the point then and there, a sudden cascade of fluid splashed down her legs, soaking her large, white maternity dress and puddling on the floor.

She gasped. 'That's... That's...'

'Your waters,' he agreed calmly. 'Did you drive here?'

'Yes.'

'And is your husband anywhere around?'

'Due back from Melbourne on a seven-thirty flight.'

'Because I don't think you should drive yourself home.'

'Home?'

'To get your hospital bag,' he soothed. 'You should get yourself admitted as soon as possible, yes, but there's time for a quick trip home. But not with you at the wheel. Once your waters break, contractions can start immediately and be quite intense.'

'Like... Like...' She wrapped her arms around her swollen belly. 'Ah-h...!'

'That. Yes,' he agreed. 'Uh, Stevie? Or Cathy? Anna?'

'Yes, Dr Marr?' Stevie said, and her gaze at once snagged deliciously on the twinkle in his eye which was meant for her alone. She had been aware of this unfolding

drama as she'd stood at the reception desk and was ready
for his summons.

'Have you ever driven a...?'

'Mitsubishi Pajero. Automatic,' Mrs Robertson supplied.

'No,' Stevie answered cheerfully, 'but I'm sure I could.'

'Good. Because I think you'd better drive her.'

The first half of the journey was uneventful. After a few
changes of direction and a few traffic lights, Stevie had
come to grips with brake, steering response and indicator,
and at four o'clock in the afternoon peak-hour traffic was
only just building.

She went as far as the front door of the house with Mrs
Robertson, then waited on the white stucco porch while the
latter produced her hospital bag, already packed and con-
scientiously filled with everything she might possibly need.
In fact, it looked heavy.

'I'll take it, Mrs Robertson,' she said.

'Under the circumstances, please, call me Deirdre!'

'Deirdre, then.'

'Yes, the bag is heavy, and I can feel another contraction...' She clutched her abdomen again and bent forward
as she almost stumbled down the steps ahead of Stevie, the
pressure of the contracting uterus forcing more amniotic
fluid out.

This time, though, it wasn't clear as it had been before.
Stevie picked up the hospital bag then watched, alarmed,
as a greenish stain began to spread down the back of the
white dress. Surely that wasn't right? Wasn't that a danger
sign?

Deirdre hadn't noticed, however, and was already climbing into the car. Her mind working frantically, Stevie
hauled the bag into the back and took the wheel again. She
had taken Ros's advice over the past few weeks and used
any spare moments at the health centre, and a bit of time

on weekends as well, to read the pamphlets provided in the waiting room and stored in Ros's office, including one quite thick booklet entitled, *You and Your Pregnancy* She was quite sure that amniotic fluid should not look like that.

I won't say anything, though. Perhaps I'm wrong. I *hope* I'm wrong, and I'd hate to panic her for nothing when her husband's away. But I'll drive as fast as I dare!

Deirdre was too absorbed in her own body to notice Stevie's darting lane changes and aggressive acceleration at each light.

'Do you know which is the maternity floor, and which is the best entrance for getting to it?' Stevie asked as they entered the hospital driveway.

'I'm not going to the maternity floor,' Deirdre said on a shallow breath. 'I'm going to the birthing centre. It's in a separate wing. All midwives, no doctors. No intervention. Of course, I can be moved quickly if there are complications, but—'

'I'd rather take you to the maternity floor,' Stevie insisted, and screeched to a stop outside Accident and Emergency. 'To...to get you registered and everything, since this is so sudden.'

It sounded lame, but she really wasn't prepared to alarm the labouring woman on the strength of her own slim knowledge. The only help her year of nursing was proving to be at this precise moment was that it increased her alarm. Fortunately, Deirdre was having another contraction and didn't argue. An orderly with a wheelchair came up as Stevie was helping Deirdre out of the car. 'Labour and delivery?'

'Yes.'

'No, this is *wrong*!' Deirdre insisted, angry now as she turned to Stevie. Her contraction had ebbed again. 'Why are you being so stupid about it? I want the birthing centre.'

'Can get there from here,' the orderly answered, and began to wheel her inside.

Abandoning the Robertson vehicle to the almost certain fate of a parking ticket, as it was parked just yards beyond the forbidding markers that sketched the approach to the ambulance bay, Stevie hurried ahead and grabbed someone she desperately hoped was a nurse.

'This woman,' she managed, already breathless with worry, 'wants to go to the birthing centre, but I think she shouldn't. The back of her dress is stained dirty green from the amniotic fluid and that's not good, is it? I think the baby is in distress.'

The uniformed young woman *was* a nurse. She waylaid the wheelchair and cheerfully asked Deirdre to stand up. She took one look at her dress, yelled for a wheeled stretcher and pressed the lift button for the fifth floor.

'What's wrong? Why isn't anybody listening?' Deirdre moaned, her voice high and angry.

'Love,' said the nurse, 'don't worry, but we've got to take you upstairs and get an obstetrician to look at you. We may need to get the baby out quickly.'

Deirdre began to hyperventilate and burst into tears.

'Are you with her? Her sister, or something?' demanded the square-shouldered young nurse of Stevie.

'No, I'm just the receptionist at the health centre. She went into—'

The lift arrived and no one wasted any time hearing the end of her sentence. Under the circumstances, she didn't mind.

I have to move the car, she thought. Poor Deirdre! She hasn't had a chance to contact her husband. I'll park and then come back. Ros and Aimee and everyone will wonder where on earth I've got to, but it can't be helped. I can catch up with filing tonight while I wait for the stop-smoking group to wind up.

It took some minutes to find the visitors' car park and walk back from it to the main building. At the labour and delivery nurses' station, the nurse there was sceptical at first when Stevie asked about Deirdre Robertson.

'But who are you? A relative?'

She had to explain fully, and the nurse, with commendable concern for security, then rang the health centre to check the story.

That was good, because in the process Ros found out the reason for Stevie's delay, and now finally the nurse was able to tell her, 'She's having an emergency Caesarean. She was lucky. Sometimes meconium staining doesn't signal a problem, but this time... Dr Blair was just about to leave, but he listened to the baby's heartbeat and whipped her straight in. There wasn't time for an epidural so she's under general.'

'She'll be very disappointed. She was hoping for a natural delivery at the birthing centre.'

'I know, but it was a critical situation.'

'And will the baby be all right? I'm going to try and contact her husband as soon as I get back to the health centre, and obviously if I can give him good news... He's in Melbourne, you see.'

'Oh, dear! What a disappointment all round!' Ward Sister Joanne Muir said. 'But as to the baby... Ask Dr Blair. This is him now.'

'That means it's over? The baby's been born? So fast!'

'It had to be. Excuse me, Dr Blair...' Sister Muir quickly outlined the situation and the obstetrician turned to Stevie.

'It's a boy.' He smiled at her confidently.

Absorbing the news, she demanded, 'But what shall I

tell the dad if I can reach him? Is the baby going to be all right?'

'He's fine. We got him out in time, and he was a good three kilos.' Julius had been right on the mark, then. 'Breathing well, good colour and reflexes. We kept that gunk in the amniotic fluid safely out of his lungs, too, which can be the real danger, even after birth. Here's my card with the number of my answering service. Get Mr Robertson to ring me as soon as you reach him. His wife was very upset before she went under.'

'I know.'

The obstetrician was already striding off down the corridor, after Stevie had just managed to notice, thanks to the name badge he wore, that his name was Alan Blair.

With the good news she had to relay, she made the five-minute walk from hospital to health centre with the wings on her feet beating effortlessly.

To find that Julius had already gone. He often finished early on Thursdays.

It was idiotic to feel so disappointed about it. From Stevie's face Ros concluded that there had been a problem with the Robertson baby and could obviously hardly steel herself to hear the news.

'Don't…keep me in suspense, Stevie. What went wrong?'

'Nothing, the baby's going to be fine,' Stevie clarified.

'Then why the face?'

'Oh, because I'd really like to reach the husband, and I don't know how,' she improvised.

'He's a patient here, too, so try his file,' Ros suggested. 'It probably has a work number listed. Ring that and see if they have a contact for him in Melbourne.'

Better than that, the receptionist at HSK Securities had a mobile phone number for Sean Robertson and was happy to pass it on. A minute later Stevie had reached him, just as his business meeting ended. He was husky-voiced at the news, took several minutes to fumble for paper and pen in order to take down Alan Blair's number, and ended fervently, 'I've got to get an earlier flight!'

Three hours later, in the middle of the evening appointment hours, Mr Robertson rang again, this time from his wife's bedside on the maternity floor. 'He's beautiful, Mrs Reid,' he told Stevie. She didn't bother to correct him as to her marital status. 'Lachlan, we've called him, and I'll pass you over to Deirdre in a minute because she wants to thank you.'

'It's thanks enough to know the baby is fine,' she told him truthfully.

'I know, but she tells me he might well not have been if you hadn't alerted the staff to the staining of her waters. We're really grateful.'

'Really, there's no need—' Stevie began, but he interrupted.

'The only thing is, do you have any idea where Deirdre's car keys have got to?'

'Oh, my goodness, they're still in my pocket!'

Unable to leave the centre now until she closed it for the night, and not wanting to drag the new father away from his wife and baby on a nuisance of an errand, Stevie promised to deliver the keys to him in the maternity unit as soon as she finished at nine. This, of course, meant that there was no way she'd be home and waiting for Julius when he arrived at twenty past.

The thought of missing him—if he came and went again because the place was dark and she didn't answer the door—swamped her with a disappointment that sent great warning bells clanging in her head. She thought, This is too dangerous! I'm getting in so deep, and so quickly.

She ignored this knowledge totally, waited impatiently until appointments had ended and it was just the stop-smoking group winding up in the meetings room with Dr McKinnon, then she found Julius's pager number on the centre's emergency contact sheet and dialled it.

He rang back within five minutes and heard the story, then promised, 'I'll meet you in Mrs Robertson's room, then, because I'd like to congratulate her and see the bub…' He lowered his voice. 'And I *wouldn't* like to have to wait an extra half an hour before I see you.'

'No. I know,' she agreed breathlessly. 'I was afraid we'd miss each other altogether.'

'Not if I can help it.'

His low voice was like a caress, but then in the background Stevie heard, very distinctly, a woman's voice calling, 'Kyle, Lauren, bedtime!'

'So…three-quarters of an hour, then?' Julius murmured again, making no comment on the background activity. 'I can't wait.'

'Neither can I,' Stevie agreed, but all of a sudden she felt a little shaky and her throat had tightened around the words.

He'd said he was going home to work on the computer. She had imagined a rather cheerless, solitary evening, fuelled by a bachelor's dinner, and had looked forward in a very female way to giving him the nourishment of warmth and companionship and cosseting tonight. But he wasn't alone at all, and if that was 'home', then who lived there with him?

A wife and children. That was the conclusion anyone would reach on the basis of those few simple words in a woman's voice—'Kyle, Lauren, bedtime!'

The first seed of doubt planted itself in Stevie's mind. She ignored it resolutely. There's an innocent explanation…not that I'll ask him for it! This is about *me*, not him, about my vulnerability because it's all so new, and because it's been so long.

All of which was true.

And then their evening together was perfect. She had returned the car keys to Mr Robertson and was admiring the baby when Julius walked in.

'Not what we'd planned, Deirdre,' he said to the new mother, 'but in a few days, when you're not so sore, it won't matter.'

'It doesn't matter now,' she answered, still a little fuzzy and washed out from anaesthesia. 'I'm sore, yes, but he's so beautiful.' Her voice broke on the word.

Julius and Stevie spent another few minutes with the proud parents and then tore themselves away, to the accompaniment of more thanks. Although they'd enjoyed the visit, it was heaven, now, to be alone. Stevie's doubts disappeared. He was looking at her as if he'd hungered for her all day, and said as he brushed a strand of russet hair from her face, 'You OK? You looked a bit tense when I first walked in.'

'I'm fine.' It was true now. 'H-how did your work go?'

He grimaced. 'Slow! Frustrating! Trying to pull eight different research papers out of a mass of data gathered over seven years is not easy. Don't make me talk about it!'

'I won't,' she answered tenderly, coming up to him as they were alone in the descending lift so that she could soothe the lines in his forehead with her fingers.

'Stevie,' he groaned, winding his arms around her. 'I strongly suspect that I—' He broke off.

'What?'

'Nothing. Nothing! That I'm going to keep you up far too late, if you'll let me.'

'I'd love it. Make me yawn all through tomorrow, please!'

He did, taking her out to supper at a smart little café in Paddington where there was live music, and then driving up to Watson's Bay so they could watch the moon over the sea…and explore their growing sensual awareness of one another in the sheltered lee of the cliff path.

The didn't talk much. Scattered phrases.

She tripped on a step she hadn't seen and he caught her and murmured, 'Careful…' He held her tightly against him, running his hand down her back, covering her mouth with his. Or trying to. They both laughed at the mutual moment of clumsiness that had her fervently kissing his chin.

It was after midnight before he brought her home, and before she could say anything…before she could decide what she *wanted* to say…he said seriously, 'Don't ask me in, Stevie. It's too late…and I want you too badly. Just let me see you again on Saturday.'

'I'm free,' she answered, breathless again. 'On Sunday afternoon I'm playing with the band, but we're not practising this weekend. Saturday is completely free.'

'Good!' he said against her mouth, but after he'd gone she mused, I sounded so horribly eager, as if I'd be willing to clear my entire schedule just to be with him.

It was true, of course. She would.

Meanwhile, solitude after her working hours ended at five on Friday afternoon brought to the fore the nagging issue of all those letters from men who subscribed to *Sydney Scene*. They still sat stacked in her desk drawer in her little study, including the one from 'call me John', annotated in her own handwriting with the words, 'Meeting for drinks—Wednesday, 5.45.'

She was tempted to fling the whole bundle in the garbage.

But ding-a-ling-a-ling went the alarm bells.

'Don't do this to yourself, Stevie,' she scolded herself aloud. '*Don't* ruin this thing with Julius by making it too important!'

Accordingly, having to steel herself to do it, she rang 'call me John' at the work number he'd put in his letter and said brightly after her greeting, 'What happened the other night? Did we miss each other somehow?'

'Look, I can't talk now,' said the man's edgy voice.

Stevie's jaw clenched and she said coolly, going with the intuition she'd had all along about this one, 'What, your wife's there, is she?'

There was a blank moment of silence and then, 'Yes. How did you know?' He was clearly too startled to soften the words, let alone think of a different answer.

'Some tactics are all too obvious,' she answered, still completely cool. 'I expect your wife is under no illusions, either...'

The phone at the other end was slammed down.

Stevie screwed the letter from 'John' into a ball and looked at the rest of her bundle with a sinking heart. I can't, she thought. I should, perhaps. Just to keep my options open. But I can't.

Not when I love Julius already.

By the end of the following week, Stevie knew she would sleep with him very soon.

They had spent the whole of Saturday together, totally involved with one another and not actually *doing* very much at all. He had come over before lunch and they'd shopped lazily at the local markets for a gourmet picnic, which they'd eaten in the back garden, lying on a blue tartan picnic rug and surrounded by the scent of Mum's late roses.

'I like shopping with you,' he'd said, so they'd done some more of it, browsing through some galleries and antique markets in the eastern suburbs. It hadn't mattered in the slightest that they hadn't bought anything, but they'd had enough exercise to feel both tired and hungry so they'd retired to her place again and had eaten take-away Chinese while they'd watched a rented movie from the video store.

'But I'd better not admit to having seen it if anyone asks, because I somehow don't feel I absorbed very much of the plot,' she told him afterwards, still lazing in his arms on the couch.

'Neither did I…'

It came out quite sleepily, and she scolded him gently, 'You should go home while you can still keep your eyes open to drive.' She knew that he had a house and that it was about twenty minutes away in Surry Hills, but no more than that.

'Should I?' The meaning behind the two laconic words was very clear.

She'd had to struggle hard to keep to a decision she'd made very deliberately before his arrival that morning.

Not yet. Don't lose yourself to him so fully just yet.

'Yes,' she said carefully. 'You should.'

It was very gentle, palpably reluctant. Many men would have seized their chance, pressed the point and won an eager capitulation quite soon, but Julius did not do that. He *did* go home, without further protest, and the little seed of doubt, still lying quiet and unacknowledged in the back of Stevie's mind, shrivelled.

If he was married and looking for an affair on the side, he'd want to get to the point of the exercise as soon as he decently could, she told herself. Like 'John', probably. If he's prepared to wait until I'm ready, until we've spent more time together, then he really does care about how I feel.

Work that week was difficult, and distraction constant.

I couldn't have been a doctor, she realized. My emotions are too close to the surface, and too apt to interfere. Doctors can't afford to be that way.

Julius wasn't. To look at him, no one would have guessed that he had just embarked on a new relationship. He was, as usual, assiduous in chasing up test results and contacting patients as soon as possible to let them know if anything was wrong.

He had two visits from pharmaceutical salesmen, too, and evidently asked such searching questions about the new products they were offering that both left with the promise that they'd look up the relevant statistics and get back to him.

And each evening he left with the same heavy briefcase that had accompanied him in the morning and the clear intention of working late at home. Stevie could not help feeling a little shut out of that part of his life. He said so little about it. But perhaps that was natural.

I don't have enough medical knowledge to make an interested audience. If anything, he needs me to take his mind *off* work, not help him dwell on it.

In theory, the idea did not displease her. There were many less desirable roles in life than to be an intelligent and successful man's helpmeet—the one who soothed his stress, gave him a world away from work and made sure he was well cared for. The idea of caring for Julius and having him care, in his different male way, for her was already the new dawn on her life's horizon.

So, yes, very soon, when he asked again if he could stay the night, her answer would be, 'Yes.'

CHAPTER FIVE

'IT REALLY would help, Irene,' Julius said, having to force patience and politeness into his tone, 'if the children weren't *always* around when we need to meet.'

He had made the suggestion as kindly as he could, but her look was still one of deep reproach, and her control, too, was thin when she finally spoke. 'Don't disappoint them, Jules.'

The nickname was years old and utterly familiar—so familiar that he'd almost forgotten how much he disliked it.

'They need their father so badly,' she went on. 'Can't you see that, every time you're with them? It doesn't take much out of your time, surely…?' Her voice had gone hard now.

There were a hundred things he could have said to that, but he managed to restrict himself instead to a simple, weary, 'Yes. Yes, I can see that, Irene.'

It was the end of a very long day. Kyle and Lauren would soon be in bed, he and Irene would cover just one or two more small issues and then he'd be free. His heart lifted. Free to see Stevie!

Irene had kept him even longer than usual today, forced dinner on him, too—a delicious, home-made chicken and almond casserole, and she had always been a superb cook.

Stevie was playing with her band tonight and wouldn't be free until after ten, which had disappointed him vastly on Thursday when she had told him. Now, it emerged as fortunate, because if she *hadn't* been playing, he'd have wanted to have had dinner with her, and to juggle that with Irene's demands would have been fraught with disaster.

'I'll deal with the children,' Irene said. 'Will you come and say goodnight to them in a few minutes, though?'

'Of course, Irene,' he answered, feeling like a mean-spirited scoundrel because, still, all he could think of was getting out of there. By nine, perhaps? He knew where Lizzy in the Kitchen was playing. He'd love to hear Stevie sing…

It was not to be. Irene summoned him to the children at eight-thirty, and by the time he'd looked at a computer game, heard another story about school, hugged them and come downstairs again Irene had the television on for her weekly fix of a long-running British police drama.

'Must you?' This time he couldn't hide his impatience.

'You know I love this…'

'Yes, but weren't we going to sort through the—?'

'Let's not. Not tonight. I've made enough decisions for today.'

She stood, as if suddenly restless, and used the remote control to extinguish the programme she'd just claimed to enjoy so much. Now she was prowling, twiddling with the dimmer switch by the door to lower the lights and pouring wine, which he didn't want. He took it, though, to have something to do with his hands, but the next minute she'd plucked the stemmed glass out of his grasp again.

'Julius… Oh, Julius…'

He should have seen it coming. The twin glasses of wine were forgotten on the coffee-table and her arms were around him, tired, trembling, needy, sensuous. Only then did he register that she'd removed her light wool jacket while he'd been upstairs with Kyle and Lauren, and wore only a black, thin-strapped silk camisole. Against its opaque inkiness, her arms were pale and soft and strong.

She'd always had beautiful arms. He remembered how, for too many years, those arms had absorbed and distracted him.

And, he now knew, she had been far too aware of the emotional and sensual power she had had over him back then, and had used it…as she was trying to use it now.

'Julius,' she whispered again, the sound a sibilance and a purr in her throat.

'Irene…' He wasn't prepared to reject her roughly. For so long he had wanted her this way.

And she was offering herself. It was patently clear, palpable, heavy in the air between them. This wasn't just a kiss for old times' sake.

'Just a few minutes,' she whispered. 'Then the children will be thoroughly asleep and we can go upstairs.' Her red mouth pouted to press softly against his. 'I know you want it as much as I do…'

Julius stirred and felt the weight of weeks of built-up fatigue still upon him. Where was he? An unfamiliar sheet covered his naked body and beside him lay the form of a woman, her hair tousled on the pillow and her ribcage rising and falling in sleep.

That's right, he realised, a hot flame of remembered desire rekindling and licking inside him. He had stayed the night.

Stretching slowly and strongly, he felt his fatigue begin to ebb and a glow of satisfaction…contentment… No, damn it, man, be honest! It was *happiness*! He felt sheer happiness seize him as he lay here beside her.

He couldn't believe how good it had felt to hold her, slide her clothes slowly down her body, touch her skin, devour her mouth, hear her ragged laughter and her cat-like purring, lie beside her, feel her beneath him, plunge into her...

And now it was bright daylight and he was still here, and she hadn't woken yet so he could gaze at her openly without having to fear anything about what he might be giving away. He'd never felt this way before. This fullness. This exultancy. This sense of coming home at last.

Then, all too soon, she stirred and opened her eyes and caught him at it. She smiled at once, still as sleepy as a cat, and he smiled back, the grin spreading helplessly across his whole face.

'Hello, Stevie,' he said.

'Hi.' Her delicious voice caught a little in her throat. 'Have you been awake long?'

'Not long. Sorry if I woke you.' He was, but admitted to himself that it was a selfish sorrow. If he could have kept watching her...

'You didn't wake me,' she told him. 'By the look of the sun, it must be late.' She peered, one eye still shut, at her alarm clock. 'Ten! My goodness! Do you have to be somewhere?'

'No,' he answered truthfully, relishing the fact.

'Then you'll stay for breakfast?'

'Call it brunch, a bit later on, and I'll say yes.'

'Brunch, then.' She frowned, not grasping his meaning. 'So, would you like a shower?'

'No, I would not like a shower,' he answered patiently.

He had showered last night at home before coming here, lengthily and obsessively, to wash Irene's scent and garish lip-gloss from his skin, which meant he'd got here late and Stevie had met him at the door, visibly...hero-ically...stifling a reproach. The thing had soon been for-gotten.

They'd stumbled to bed, arm in arm, at about one

o'clock. But the last thing he felt like now was another shower! Amongst other reasons, hers was a scent he *wanted* on his skin!

She understood now, and he loved the sight of the pretty colour that crept into her cheeks. 'Oh…' she said.

Neither of them spoke any intelligible words for nearly an hour…

Lying in his arms afterwards, Stevie felt happier than she'd been in her life. Last night, knowing from even before his arrival that she would ask him to stay, she had been jittery and tense. It had been a huge step. It had meant so much. There had been so much room for failure, regret, misery.

She had never been particularly compatible with Grant in bed and had ignored the problem back then, talked herself out of it. She'd been too young to realise just what it had meant and how deeply it had run.

Now, fifteen years on, she knew how important it was, and felt that if she and Julius could not connect in this most intimate and private way, then that would send out fatal signals about the relationship.

But within an hour of his arrival last night, those worries had vanished. He was an astonishing lover. Ardent, patient, tender, bold, sensitive, inventive… They had reached heights of passion together which she had not known were possible, and she still felt like jelly and silk and cream all over, inside and out, as a result.

If anything, this morning…just now…had been even better. They'd jumped the big hurdle of the first time last night. Now, with no pressure, Stevie could surrender herself utterly to sensation, moved beyond belief by his devotion to her pleasure. She felt absolutely no desire for food. This was enough nourishment to the senses, this warm, replete laziness here in bed.

If time stopped…if the world ended in some cosmic explosion at this moment…I'd hardly mind, she thought.

Finally, though, it was time to return to everyday reality just a little. Tall, well-built males who'd recently expended considerable energy in love-making and hadn't eaten in nearly twelve hours got hungry.

They dressed casually then slopped around the kitchen together, squeezing orange juice, making coffee and cooking a full breakfast of eggs and bacon, sausages and tomatoes, grilled mushrooms, baked beans and toast. Stevie began to envisage the possibility of having someone to cook for who really appreciated his food.

In the afternoon they went to Maroubra Beach and took a long walk north as far as Coogee and back again, barefoot as the waves broke up to their calves in the shallows. They ate ice cream, sitting in Coogee's grassy beachside park, and walked back again.

At her place, they sealed the day with another unbrookable outpouring of passion—Stevie had never made love on the carpet before, with only afternoon sunlight blanketing their tangled limbs—and then Julius said with frank regret as he held her against his naked, rugged chest, 'I can't stay any longer, Stevie. I shouldn't have *stayed* this long. There's a huge pile of stuff I have to get through tonight.'

'Nothing that I could help you with?' she said eagerly. 'Typing, or…'

She felt foolish when he shook his head at once and said quickly, 'It'd take longer to explain what you needed to do than it would take me to actually do it, I'm afraid.'

'It's your research, isn't it? Not something connected with the health centre. What's it about?'

'You don't want to know.'

'Yes, I do!'

'Well, the original goal of the study was to examine genetic versus environmental factors in the incidence of certain childhood diseases, but we found as we progressed that—' He stopped and shook his head. '*Please*, don't make me talk about this!'

'OK.'

'You see at the moment I'm so—'

'Overdosed on it,' she completed for him. 'I know. So don't talk about it. I understand. Just don't ever make the mistake of presuming I'm not interested, that's all, and if you ever do need to talk…to get something off your chest…'

He gave a rather hollow laugh. 'Bless you for that, Stevie. Bless you…'

He left soon afterwards, and the house might have seemed empty if her thoughts hadn't filled it so powerfully with his presence.

They had both agreed that it was important to say nothing at work about what was happening between them. Stevie didn't question Julius's feelings on the subject, since she fully shared them.

The last thing she wanted at this stage was curiosity and conjecture, no matter how well-meaning. There was no sinister reason for secrecy, of course, none at all, but the relationship was new and fragile and too precious to risk bruising.

It was only natural that Julius would share this feeling, and it was quite delicious, in many ways, to catch his eye during the day and see that special glint in it, reserved only for her.

When Cathy Hong asked on Wednesday, in her lightly accented English, whether Stevie was enjoying the job so far, the enthusiasm of the latter's response was probably quite astonishing.

Stevie had completely forgotten—if, with Grant, she had ever truly known—what it felt like to spend time with a man you loved. The delicious laziness of it. The way the most routine of activities suddenly became special and new again when you did them together—showering, washing the dishes, reading the paper. The fascination of finding out more and more about each other—tastes and interests shared, piquant differences, fresh, intriguing viewpoints.

'I just wish this wasn't happening right at the time when you're *so* busy with your research work,' she told him as they lay in bed one rainy evening a week and a half after their first explosive night together.

He shifted uncomfortably. 'I know. So do I.'

'But it has to come to an end soon, doesn't it?'

'Soon…' he echoed. 'At least, I wish I could say that with more confidence. You may have to be prepared…for some broken promises, Stevie.'

At the time, she took the line at face value, and assumed that he'd meant rendezvous that didn't happen. Curtailed meals. A phone call instead of a planned meeting.

But that innocence didn't last long, she reflected just a few days later.

It began on a Friday, when there was more rain, and Sydney's reputation as a sunny city was in grave danger of collapsing and washing away into one of the swollen, tea-coloured, storm-water drains.

A lot of people came into the health centre with complications from colds and flu, including an older gay couple who seemed very devoted to each other and referred to each other constantly as 'my partner'.

That seemed to be the word of choice these days, Stevie reflected, for people of either gender who weren't actually married but wanted to signal to the rest of the world that they had a long-term, close-knit and committed relationship. It was at least the third time she'd heard it this week from patients.

But I don't think it would be quite enough for me. It sounds too cool and businesslike. And, of course, she was thinking of Julius, heaven help her!

The two men left with prescriptions for antibiotics and strong cough medicine, and then poor Sally Kitchin was back again, her triplets now over three months old. Sally had only half-heartedly taken up the offer of help which Stevie had made some weeks earlier. She'd accepted two hours of help with house-cleaning, and that had been that.

'Michael is back in a week. I'm fine, really, thanks, Stevie.'

But now Sally's husband was away again and the babies were once more engaged in a chorus of crying that had grown louder and stronger since their last visit. They were growing, and clearly all had nice, powerful lungs. Sally had got here early. It was five to eleven, and her appointment was not until ten past.

Making an imprint of her Medicare card while the three babies lay in their triple-sized pram, Stevie almost tried a joke on the subject, but something in the new mother's face stopped her. She really looked wrung out.

She watched as Sally sat down again by the pram. She rocked the wheels back and forth gently but the crying continued. Sally seemed oblivious to the sound.

The rest of the waiting patients certainly weren't, however, and the chorus of howls soon began to grate on everyone's nerves. An older man began to look daggers at Sally, and two women whispered to each other that *they* had never let *their* babies cry in public. Mothers these days had no consideration for others…

Stevie felt her own tension mounting. She had asked Sally which one was the patient today, and Sally hadn't even seemed to know. 'Amelia,' she had said vaguely. 'Amelia, I suppose.' But she was taking no more notice of Amelia than of James or Nicholas.

Mr Pye, the man with the dagger-like expression, came up to the desk and said loudly, 'Can't you do something about those dreadful babies? There should be a separate waiting room for children. Why do *we* have to put up with it?'

Stevie was tempted to ask him rather bluntly how often *he'd* had to look after three babies at once for even a few minutes, let alone day and night, but managed to say mildly instead, 'Dr Irwin will be ready to see you any minute, Mr Pye, and then it won't be your concern.'

He grunted.

The two women were evidently having a change of heart. They came up to the desk and asked Stevie in a whispered chorus, 'Do you think she'd mind if we held them and soothed them? Poor thing!'

'Triplets *would* be a handful! When I think back on it, we did have some dreadful days.'

'You can feel quite helpless!'

'I don't suppose she'd mind,' Stevie began, then looked past the women to Sally. She had stood up, her face still blank and staring, and was fumbling in her bag, muttering aloud about cash for the bus. Then she began to head for the door.

Everyone began to stare and whisper, and Stevie felt a pang of real alarm. 'Actually, ladies,' she said quickly, 'I think I'll get Sally and her babies settled somewhere private.'

When she went over, she almost had to drag Sally back from the door, as well as wheeling the pram by herself.

'What's the matter, Sally?' she asked, as soon as they were alone.

The young mother immediately burst into tears as well. Stevie was a great believer in the therapeutic value of a lot of tearful noise, so she didn't try to soothe Sally into silence but simply gave her a big hug and said, 'Just let it all out...'

The babies themselves seemed so shocked at their mother encroaching on their own vocal territory in this way that they all settled down to a whimper and then two of them went to sleep.

There was a knock at the door, and Aimee poked her silvery head around it. She was a delightful woman, Stevie had found by this time, and everyone was feeling slightly disloyal in their disappointment that she would be leaving soon. She was in the process of looking for a permanent job. Nurse Bronwyn Hurst, currently on maternity leave and due to return in the last week of May, just wasn't quite as nice!

Aimee said, 'Sally, love, I've brought you some tea, and bottles and nappies for the babies. I noticed you'd forgotten your baby bag.'

'Oh, I know.' Sally sniffed, calmer now. 'There's a very large hole opened up in my brain somehow.'

Now Julius appeared in the doorway as well. 'Ready, Sally?'

She took a gulp of tea, then nodded.

'Ear infections again, in James and Amelia,' Julius told Stevie fifteen minutes later when she brought him his mid-morning coffee. She had a cup for Rebecca Irwin, too, and would deliver that next.

'These three seem prone to them. That's the third time, isn't it?'

'Yes, it is. Unfortunately some babies just are. I pre-scribed a different antibiotic this time, and I'll have them in for follow-up at the end of the course to make sure it's completely gone. Some children end up having a drain put in for a few years until they outgrow the problem, but hopefully we won't have to go that far in this case. I'm also wondering…' He hesitated. 'Do you see much of Sally over the back fence?'

'Not lately.' I've been seeing too much of *you*! 'She's pretty independent. We're not close enough friends for her to feel comfortable about taking my help, unfortunately.'

'You see, I'm becoming a little concerned about the possibility of postnatal depression.'

'But wouldn't she bring that up herself?'

'No, very often women don't. They don't recognise that what they're feeling goes beyond the normal fatigue and baby blues, or they're ashamed to admit to it. After all, they've generally been told it's supposed to be the happiest time of their lives.'

'Which for many women it is.'

'Everyone's different. Different circumstances. Different expectations.'

'Sally doesn't get enough support, I think.'

'Her husband is putting his career first—for commendable reasons, I expect, but the result is the same.'

'So you're asking me to…'

'Drop in and see her. Tell me how things seem at home. I'll go myself next week, but two visits and two opinions would give a better picture. I don't want to jump the gun on this—but I don't want her to suffer unnecessarily either. I was concerned that she seemed too vague and detached today, as well as tearful… By the way, I love your dress. It does gorgeous things to your hair.'

The *non sequitur* was so delicious that Stevie gave a peal of laughter—quickly suppressed as she considered the impression it would create on any listeners beyond the office door.

'Thank you,' she said. 'And I *will* make sure to see Sally. But I must get this coffee to Dr Irwin before it goes tepid on me.'

Going tepid… Something which was not a remote danger as far as her feelings for Julius went. The only thing worse than not seeing him in the busy course of the day was the scattered glimpses she did catch of the man as he came and went between patients. Tantalising, frustrating glimpses, impossible to relish and enjoy because of the fact that no one else at the health centre knew about them.

By the end of this tiring Friday morning, Stevie was so taut-nerved that she almost gave the whole thing away as she watched Julius go off to lunch, by rushing after him to say, I can skip my errands. Can't you skip yours and we'll eat together? We're hardly going to see each other this weekend…

Lizzy in the Kitchen had four engagements, an unusually heavy schedule, and Julius had a lot of work to catch up on, too. 'Because I've been…distracted three nights this week,' he'd said to her yesterday evening when they'd discussed weekend plans.

In the end, though, she let him disappear out the staff door in the direction of the car park without saying anything. Best to be sensible, even when you felt so giddy and silly and happy and…just wonderful.

The phone rang and she answered it automatically with the crisp, cheerful, 'Southshore Health Centre,' that was now second nature.

'Look, I need to get hold of Julius Marr urgently and he's not answering his direct line *or* his mobile,' said a harried woman's voice.

'I think he's just on his way to his car now,' Stevie

answered. 'If you try again in a minute or two, you should get him on the mobile.'

'All right, but if I don't can you please give him a message?'

'Of course.'

'Just tell him I'm having a problem with—' She stopped. 'No, don't worry. Just tell him I rang.'

'And you are…?'

'Irene. And *you* are…?'

'Stephanie Reid.'

'Stephanie? I see. Well, I'm his partner. So do see that he's told, will you, Stephanie?' The phone clicked at the other end and then began to burr in Stevie's ear. She felt sick and miserable and full of foreboding.

Stubborn, too!

I'm being paranoid, she thought, as she left a brief, formal message on his desk, written deliberately in neat capitals so he would not think to wonder whose writing it was. IRENE RANG.

He's *not* a dishonest man! Surely I have enough confidence in my judgement of character to know that! I've known from the beginning that a man like Julius doesn't reach the age of forty-two without leaving some kind of an emotional entanglement behind him. 'Partner' is such a catch-all term! Yes, I really don't like it! She may be using it to mean they're about to be divorced, or something. After all, she could hardly have said, 'his nearly ex-wife'.

Of course I'm upset that he hasn't chosen to talk to me about it yet, but he's quite a private man in many ways. And he needs his space. Look at the way he so dislikes discussing his research.

The rationalisations were pitifully easy to create, and Stevie wanted desperately for them to make sense. At the same time, though, she knew she had to talk to him about Irene.

We've only been involved for a few weeks but, still, at some point I have a right to ask, and a right to know...

CHAPTER SIX

THE afternoon, their schedule and their colleagues conspired to prevent any time alone together, however.

Julius was late back from lunch, his head and shoulders spattered with raindrops, and he had two patients already waiting so that even the brief snatch of conversation they managed to share was stolen.

'You look tired and strung out,' he said to Stevie, leaning over the desk so that she caught a brief wafting tendril of the male scent she loved on him so much.

'I am,' she admitted in answer to his gentle accusation. 'And I wish so much that we were seeing each other this weekend!'

'I know,' he agreed. 'You'll have to tell that band of yours—'

'It's not just the band,' she cut in quite tartly. '*Your* schedule is just as much at fault!'

The accusation seemed to catch him like a blow and his strong jaw tightened against it as he left the front desk and strode down the corridor to his office without another word.

She hated herself for hours afterwards. He'd been teasing. Why had she felt the need to bite back like that, and at a time when it couldn't possibly be followed through? A sense of vulnerability did terrible things to your behaviour in a relationship.

But by the time I can apologise, an apology would only make things worse. It was a stupid thing to say, but I won't bring it up again. I just have to let it slide.

They barely had the opportunity to speak for the rest of

the day, and he left as soon as his office hours were finished, with his briefcase and his frown both firmly in place.

He never frowns when we're together, Stevie thought, taking comfort in it.

She was busy herself that night, having time only to go home and change before heading off on an absurdly long drive to reach the far-western Sydney suburb where the band was playing that night.

The traffic was terrible and she thought irritably as she waited behind a string of large trucks, was it Alex who accepted this gig? We really shouldn't play at places that are an hour and a half's drive from *all* of us!

And on top of the traffic, a difficult set-up, and a sketchy dinner, their performance was not particularly well received either. The large group of surly high-schoolers were evidently *not* country music fans. This had been the principal's idea for the biannual school dance, not theirs, and they made the fact very apparent.

Lizzy in the Kitchen had been contracted to perform for two hours, however, so perform they did.

'Well, *that* did heaps for my professional ego!' Lizzy herself said at the end.

She looked horribly tired, and actually panted and sweated as she packed up her drum kit and wheeled it towards the van, although she took frequent rests.

'Is everything all right, Lizzy?' Stevie asked, concerned. At forty-five, with two teenagers of seventeen and fourteen and an endless round of committees and working bees and rosters, as well as playing in the band, Lizzy was normally tireless and cheerful.

'I just need a good night's sleep,' she answered, forcing a brighter expression on her face.

'Are you sure?'

'OK. A good *year's* sleep.'

She had lost weight lately, too, Stevie realised, although doubtless Lizzy would consider that a good thing.

'Well, make sure you at least get tonight,' Stevie said gently.

'Don't worry! I'm planning to!'

So was Stevie, but it didn't happen. For a start, it was midnight by the time she got home, and the long day had left her with jangling nerves that wouldn't settle straight away. She went dutifully to bed but tossed and turned for so long that she finally got up again, found a book and made herself some hot chocolate.

From the kitchen window she could see a glint of light across the corner of the back fence. It looked as if Sally Kitchin was awake, too, with one of her babies. Maybe all three.

Get yourself a hot drink, too, Sally, Stevie thought. It helps...

Definitely! To sit up cosily in bed and read and sip until she felt drowsy. Most people felt drowsy at two after rising at seven...

Most people then slept in *beyond* seven the next morning. Stevie did not, however. She woke with all the snap of a piece of toast popping up, and though she'd have liked nothing more than to doze off again she knew it wouldn't happen.

I'm thinking about Julius... I'm thinking about that woman on the phone yesterday. Irene. And that ridiculous word 'partner'. I hate it! I'm wondering... How can I help wondering? If his relationship with her a lot murkier and a lot more complex than I want to believe? Divorce *is* hard. It's not like cancelling a credit card. Even if the two of them were never legally married—maybe *that's* why she used the word—the practical and emotional fall-out can go on for years. And as for the children...

*　　*　　*

The children.

Julius had almost come to hate weekends these days because of Lauren and Kyle, and yet he felt horribly guilty about resenting the time he was forced to spend with them. He kept searching for other solutions. There *were* other solutions! But he never had the heart to present them to Irene because she was so vulnerable now, so very close to not coping at all.

He felt trapped by her vulnerability, which, again, made him feel guilty, and he *ached* physically, spiritually, in *every* way, to be with Stevie this weekend. In comparison with Irene, she always seemed to him to be so very strong, her emotions clear and frank and without manipulative intent.

Odious things, comparisons, and yet he could hardly help making them between the two women in his life. His *double* life, he amended as he rolled out of bed, accepting that sleep would not return. His horrible double life.

Stupid! It was only just after seven, and he hadn't arrived home until after two. He wasn't due to meet Irene again until ten so he had plenty of time, but sleep had flown all the same. He showered, washing his hair, then shaved and dressed casually, feeling fresher now but no more positive about the day ahead.

His double life…and he cherished no illusions, at the moment, about which part of it he preferred.

Stevie would soon have to know about Irene. Anything else was rapidly becoming dishonest and unfair, and yet he shrank from telling her. Irene was far from being finished with him.

Indeed, he knew she had still greater demands yet to make and, though there was one demand he would not accede to under any circumstances, some of the others might yet earn his reluctant acquiescence.

After all, the career that had meant everything to him for so long was at stake, and Irene had the power to sabotage it all. Oh, not intentionally. He knew her too well to suspect her of that. In some areas of her life she was far more manipulative and controlling than he would at one time have believed, but in other areas she was far less so.

Stevie, on the other hand, was not manipulative at all, just delightfully honest and open and fresh. So open, in fact, that he'd had no trouble in reading yesterday afternoon that she was tense and upset, and he still hoped to make contact with her this weekend to see if anything was wrong, although they'd agreed on Thursday night that it wouldn't be possible.

Now, for instance...

But, no, it was still only seven-thirty. She'd have got home late last night and would be sleeping in. The last thing he wanted was to wake her, when they didn't have time to see each other, and talk about Irene over the phone. If only he'd found out yesterday where she was playing!

Reluctantly he accepted that in order to be really alone ith her, at a time when they could have as long as they wanted and could shut out the whole world, talk for hours if necessary, he'd have to wait after all, as they'd agreed, until Monday night.

'This is the *last* time that we book four shows in one weekend!'

Alex voiced what they all felt as they set up on the improvised outdoor stage at ten o'clock on Saturday morning. This time it was Jennie's daughter's school fête they were playing at, set up in the spacious grounds of the exclusive girls' school she attended in the eastern suburbs.

'How on earth did we let it happen?' Stevie agreed.

'Mixed-up calendars,' Alison, the fifth member of the

group, supplied. 'Don't you remember? We accepted the high school show because we thought it was March, and when they clarified the date we didn't want to back out.'

'I wonder if we need to stop playing for things like this,' Stevie mused aloud.

'Things like what?' said Jennie.

'Things to oblige people we know.'

There was a chorus of protest. 'But those are the ones I really *like* doing!' Alex said.

'If we're going to thin out our schedule—' Jennie came in.

'We are!'

'Then it's places like Coravale High School *I'd* leave off the list!'

'Oh, so would I,' Stevie agreed.

'Well, where *do* we play, according to you?' Jennie was belligerent and, like all of them, short-tempered.

Everyone was tired, and everyone was resenting that what had always been fun was starting to turn into a chore. Stevie tried to fight her way through to a positive resolution on the issue.

'I think what we're all feeling,' she said, 'is that there needs to be a consensus on how much we want to play and what events are our top priorities. When we practise next week, let's make an official policy. I know *I'm* finding it tough with a full-time job now.'

'And I just *have* to get more involved with my kids' school,' said Alison. 'This weekend is crazy! Wayne nearly had a fit about me being out so much. Yes, let's make a policy, and stick to it!'

The only person who wasn't joining in, Stevie noticed, was Liz. She was putting together her drum kit and, as yesterday, was making very heavy work of it. After studying her covertly for some minutes, Stevie finally said to her when no one else was in earshot, 'Are you feeling unwell, Lizzy?'

'Just tired.'

'More than that,' she insisted, seeing her old friend with sudden clarity. Liz looked quite ill with fatigue. 'Perhaps you should see a doctor.'

'You know, Stephanie, ever since you've started working at the health centre you think everyone should see a doctor at every possible opportunity,' Liz snapped. 'Are you getting a cut of the proceeds or something?'

It was grossly unfair.

Stevie had made such a suggestion precisely once before this—to Alex when she'd had a heavy cough which hadn't been clearing. That had been severe bronchitis, for which a strong antibiotic had been needed.

For a moment Liz's words were like a slap in the face, then she realised inwardly, Liz is really scared. That's why she's reacting so aggressively and why she's trying to hide her fatigue and weight loss from other people. She knows in her heart that something *is* wrong, and she's too scared of what it might be.

She took a deep breath and said aloud, deliberately blunt, 'If it's something serious, wouldn't it be better to know *now*?'

But this approach didn't work.

'There's nothing wrong with me that a few nights of good sleep wouldn't cure,' said Lizzy emphatically and angrily. 'So could you please leave the subject alone, Stephanie?'

Stevie swallowed her own rising anger…and her hurt. 'Sure. OK,' she agreed briefly, then turned away to hide her tight expression. What a mess!

And it was time to start warming up…

Not to put too fine a point on it, Lizzy in the Kitchen

played abysmally that day. With tempers tight and bodies and voices tired, with last night's disdainful response to their performance and the knowledge of two more shows still to come, and with an inadequate sound system and a poor location for the temporary stage, it was a distinct temptation to all of them to give up then and there.

They played five songs, then took a break for lunch and came back for half a dozen more, a preplanned set of numbers which they thought worked best in an informal outdoor setting where most people just paused for a few minutes to listen rather than taking in the whole show.

As far as the school was concerned, however, the fête looked like a success. The weather was co-operating today, sunny and mild, with one of Sydney's fabulous blue skies, and there were crowds of people milling around the stalls, queuing for rides, trying their luck at games and tasting an array of foodstuffs ranging from fairy floss to chicken ke babs.

It was only during their third last number that one family of four—two adults and a boy and girl of primary school age—suddenly stood out from the crowd and caught Stevie's attention. The children were fair-haired, well dressed, excited, and clutching strips of tickets for the rides. The mother was blonder than the children, attractive and just a little plump, and the father was…Julius.

Stevie knew the song she was singing like the back of her hand. She ought to, since she had written it herself. It was a deliberately overwrought country-style lament about shotgun weddings, unpaid bills and 'rain comin' in through the roof so hard, we would have been drier standin' out in the yard'.

Nonetheless, she dried up just before this Shakespearean couplet, and if Alex and Jennie hadn't raised their voices to compensate, the end of the verse would have been lost.

Julius hadn't seen her. To him, the music of the band was evidently just background noise, and he hadn't even looked at the stage. He appeared to be arguing with the boy, Kyle—'Kyle, Lauren, bedtime!' echoed in Stevie's head—about whether the tickets were good for the flying-fox ride.

Switching her entire performance to automatic pilot, Stevie kept watching them as she sang. The woman—it had to be Irene—kept plucking at Julius, getting his attention, straightening his collar, asking for some coins, her touch possessive and familiar. Now the girl, who must be Lauren, was doing it, too, jumping up and down and dragging on his arm.

'Oh, ple-e-a-ase!' Stevie heard distinctly above the band's music, in a child's cajoling whine.

If that's a family in the midst of a divorce, she thought, then human nature has changed an awful lot since I woke up this morning!

They looked idyllically nuclear enough to feature in a political advertising campaign or a margarine commercial. Irene and the children seemed totally dependent on Julius, and he was giving every appearance of happily providing for them.

Kyle was off to the flying fox ride. Lauren was lining up to buy a set of over-decorated knick-knack boxes from the craft stall, and Irene had her coins from Julius's pocket. She was moving towards the kebab stall now, evidently intending to provision the family with lunch.

Julius was now alone, and Stevie accidentally started on the verse about the 'rain comin' in through the roof' all over again.

After a couple of false steps, the rest of the band obediently followed her. Julius had registered the country music rhythm and melody at last. He had turned towards the stage. He had seen her...

And looked—and what a damning, tell-tale expression it was—utterly horrified and utterly guilty.

The 'rain comin' in' number ended at last, and immediately segued into their raunchy penultimate song. Stevie looked everywhere but at Julius and began to sing better than she'd ever sung in her life, out of sheer, searing desperation. Cold comfort, that was. Inside, her heart was crumbling like a piece of stale chocolate.

CHAPTER SEVEN

STEVIE.

It wasn't such a coincidence. She'd told him she was singing at the school fête of one of the band member's daughters, and this was where Lauren went to school, too—a very expensive private girls' school overlooking the water in one of Sydney's well-moneyed eastern suburbs.

But in the moment Julius saw her standing there, heard her voice falter and read her stricken expression, he knew the enormity of the error he'd made in not telling Stevie sooner about Irene.

She had it wrong, of course. It was only too easy to imagine how she must be busily misinterpreting everything she had just seen. But he could scarcely blame her for that.

If only he'd told her! He'd been put off by the complexity of it, by the grey areas. A woman like Stevie probably found it hard to deal with grey areas. To her, honourable and courageous as she was, life came far more clearly parcelled into black and white.

But he should have realised that the existence of grey areas was exactly *why* she needed to be told sooner rather than later.

Instead, however, he'd tried to keep his two lives apart until he reached the point where the past impinged less on the future, where he felt—and would be—more free. He had thought that would be best...most considerate...for Stevie and, if he was honest, easiest for himself. He had been badly wrong.

If she understands straight away, when I've told her ev-

114

erything, then I'll be luckier than I deserve, Julius thought
starkly, gritting his teeth.

Once again, as he had this morning, he began to madly
plot the possibility of seeing her today…tomorrow at the
latest. But again he realised that it just wasn't possible. This
evening's show and the one tomorrow were both at places
on the north shore, she had told him, near where one of the
band members lived, so Stevie had been invited to stay the
night with her.

And from his own point of view, if some hours of work
did not get done tonight, then the deadline for submitting
a major article to the relevant medical journal would pass,
and he was stubbornly determined that no more such set-
backs would happen. Through no fault of his own, there
had been too many of them already.

Belatedly, and angrily now, he strode off after Irene in
the direction of the kebab stall. 'After we've eaten these,'
he said, 'we must leave. I just can't go on *doing* this, Irene!'

And he didn't care about the brimming reproach and accusation that he saw in her eyes.

'Boy, you really pepped us up at the end there!' Alex told
Stevie as they began to pack up their gear. 'What happened?'

'What should have happened at the beginning,' she answered crisply. 'If we're going to hire ourselves out as a
professional band, we need to play that way!'

'Hey!' said Jennie. 'Haven't we all agreed that this weekend is too much? We *do* play to a professional standard
generally. Let's pull ourselves together a bit, gals, and stop
griping!'

Liz wasn't griping at the moment. She wasn't saying
anything at all. Instead, after clinging to the largest of her

hefty drums, she quietly sank onto the planking of the makeshift stage and lay there in a limp, sweating heap.

Stevie was the first to reach her, while Alex seized the still-active microphone and announced in a voice that wasn't quite calm enough, 'Is there a doctor present, please? One of our band members has been taken ill. Could we please have a doctor on the performance platform as soon as possible?'

Liz's eyes swam open and Stevie saw at once that they were full of fear. 'My God, Liz,' she breathed. 'See a doctor!'

'I'm fine.' She tensed her muscles as if about to rise, then slumped again. 'I *will* be fine, if I take a couple more minutes to—'

'Hell, but you're stubborn!' Stevie snarled, throwing their whole friendship on the line, too scared to do anything else. 'Liz,' she urged, gripping her friend's feeble arm. 'If it's cancer, isn't it better to find out? One thing I've learned since starting at Southshore…'

Liz rasped an angry sigh between her teeth.

Stevie pressed on, as stubborn as her friend. 'Is that there are a whole lot more health problems out there than *I'd* ever heard of before. Most of them are manageable, even if they're not curable, and surprisingly few of them will actually kill you. It's *always* best to know!'

'Look, I don't even have a doctor! I'm as healthy as a horse. You haven't got kids. You don't know. I'm *tired*, OK? And hot. And thirsty. That's *all*!'

'Stay there,' Stevie ordered bluntly. 'I'll get you a drink. Alex has paged for a doctor.'

She hoped Julius had already gone. There would be other doctors here today…

*　　*　　*

Irene was urging Julius forward, not comprehending his reluctance.

He knew quite well he was hoping someone else would get there first. If he responded to the band member's announcement, which he and Irene had both heard clearly, he'd have to confront Stevie at the worst possible moment for both of them.

'Come *on*, Julius!' Irene was saying. 'It may well be urgent.'

'You're just as much a doctor as I am, Irene,' he retorted, even while starting towards the stage, as, in his heart, he knew he had to do. But his words were puerile to his own ears, and he hated himself for creating this situation.

'I'm not, and you know it,' she told him. 'I haven't practised day-to-day medicine in over twelve years! Whereas you...'

'I know.' He nodded, accepting the inevitable and quickening his pace further. 'I'm going. Don't worry.'

'We'll meet you at the car in an hour.'

'An *hour*?'

Irene shrugged carelessly. 'It may take you that long. And anyway, the kids will be so disappointed if we leave this soon...'

She was disappearing in the direction of the flying-fox ride even as she spoke, and he had almost reached the stage. Clattering up the makeshift steps, he soon saw just what he'd expected to see—a white-faced Stevie on her knees beside one of the band members, while the other three stood around anxiously.

He reached the group just seconds before an older man, whom he recognised as one of Sydney's top plastic surgeons. The man immediately deferred to him. 'You don't mind, do you?' James Dennie drawled. 'Emergency medicine's not my area, and I hate bruising my weekends...'

'I can handle it, I think,' Julius growled, and Dr Dennie melted away at once.

The woman was conscious. She even summoned a smile. So why was Stevie looking so pale and strained?

Because of me?

His gut twisted painfully, and he tried to touch her, but she swayed away from him and he could scarcely blame her.

'I'm *just tired*!' said the woman lying in front of him.

'Let's just check a couple of things, shall we?'

'Liz's pulse feels very fast to me,' Stevie told him tightly.

'My God, you were taking my *pulse*? I thought you were holding my hand!' Liz Hancock said.

'I *was*, Liz, but I could feel—'

Something was going on here, Julius realized at once. The band's drummer looked far more than just 'tired', but, like many generally healthy people, she had a vast capacity for resistance when it came to accepting the possibility of illness.

'I really would like to take a good look at you, Ms Hancock,' he said to her carefully. 'There's a bit of a bug going round…'

He saw the relief in her eyes. 'Just a bug? Glandular fever, or something?'

'Something like that,' he soothed, his tone matter-of-fact. 'Sometimes these things just creep up on you…'

While wishing it was any doctor on earth but Julius Marr, Stevie had to concede that he was handling Lizzie's stubbornness with marvellous tact and perception. He examined her carefully, pausing to let Stevie help her sit up and give her the long glass of water Jennie had procured.

When he'd finished, he didn't say much. 'Things aren't

looking quite right'—that was his verdict. 'Could Stevie make an appointment for you to come in next week?'

'No, she could not!'

'But—'

'If it's a bug, then tell me what it is. It's bound to clear up on its own. If it's not, then I'm just tired and the only thing that's really bothering me is this splinter I got in my hand when I fell down!'

'A splinter I can deal with, if someone has tweezers,' Julius said mildly. His dark glance skated past Stevie's, but didn't linger there.

Alex produced tweezers from a small make-up kit in her bag and he was able to coax the splinter out with scarcely a wince from Liz. She remained as stubborn as ever about the more serious cloud over her health, however.

Julius departed, as there was nothing more he could do without Liz's co-operation, and the band finished packing up. Jennie managed to convince Liz not to help.

Stevie was glad of the extra work. She felt badly hurt at the rift which had opened between herself and Liz...and hurt didn't even begin to describe what she felt about Julius.

Somehow, however, she got through the weekend. The band was well received at their two remaining venues. Sheer exhaustion forced a good night's sleep on Stevie, too, at Alison's pleasant house in Lindfield.

Packing up after the performance on Sunday afternoon Lizzy said awkwardly to her, 'Look, I...I'm not angry with you, OK? I'm just... I'm sure your Dr Marr is right and it's just some little virus. It'll clear up on its own soon.'

'He's not *my* Dr Marr,' Stevie said, too quickly.

'Oh, well, sure, but you know what I mean.'

Liz was too caught up in her clumsy apology to wonder about the hasty quibble, and her words didn't fully heal the rift, only papered it over. Stevie still felt that Liz was being very foolish, and far too stubborn for her own good.

On Monday morning Stevie settled down to get through a day at Southshore Health Centre which she knew would be long and difficult.

'We need to talk, don't we?' That was all Julius had a chance to say to her as he arrived. 'May I pick you up at your place at six, as we arranged on Thursday?'

'All right,' she agreed as neutrally as she could.

He seemed satisfied with that, which angered her. I'm burning with hurt and jealousy, and he looks as if he thinks a few quick words will make it all better and I'll just fold myself obediently into his arms again.

The trouble with falling in love at nearly forty was that you had half a lifetime of experience—your own and other people's—to frighten you when things went wrong. Her long-ago engagement to Grant came back to haunt Stevie that day, as did every story she'd ever heard of marital infidelity and two-timing men.

There were many women who were quite prepared to start a relationship with a man who hadn't quite finished with the last one, but Stevie knew she was not such a woman. She was the all-or-nothing type.

Julius must clear his emotional desk before he takes me on as his next project, she thought tightly. And he *must* have known I'd feel this way or he'd have told me about Irene already, not left me to find out by chance in the way I did.

Just how long would he have tried to fool me with this 'important research' business? And just how long would he have succeeded, with me dutifully believing him, worrying about his level of overwork, not pressing for details about what he was doing?

I wonder how many other women he's tried it on? And I wonder if Irene is being fooled in the same way? Perhaps their relationship is as solid as it ever was, and I'm just one more in a passing parade. After all, what proof do I have that he's involved in medical research at all?

By the time she reached home at five-thirty that evening and readied herself for him, she was angrier than she'd been since Grant had given his callous ultimatum about choosing her mother or him—*angrier*, actually, even more deeply hurt, and in no mood to listen patiently to a self-serving interpretation of the situation from a man who had his hidden agenda hanging out a mile.

Julius would be left in no doubt about the fact that it was up to him to make the running…

And when it happened, the whole scene was every bit as unpleasant as she had feared, and more painful even that she'd been steeling herself for.

Meeting him at the door…deliberately delaying her response to the bell, although she'd been pacing nervously for the past five minutes awaiting the sound. She ducked his attempt to kiss her, then felt the unbearably familiar wash of his fresh male scent in her nostrils.

She ached for just what she believed to be so impossible and so unacceptable, a few easy words from him that would make everything suddenly all right—Irene is my sister. She's been living with me while she gets her life under control after a nasty divorce.

He didn't say it, of course, and she had known he wouldn't because it wasn't true. The guilt in his face, sticking out like a sore thumb, told her that, and the fact that he didn't even begin to pretend that nothing was wrong.

'Stevie,' he began at once, 'there are obviously some things I should have told you.'

'You've got *that* right!'

'But I didn't want to complicate things from the very beginning for us by—'

'Complicate things for *you*, you mean,' she cut in tartly.

'All right,' he conceded with a crisp lift of his strong chin, as if he'd just taken a blow there without flinching. 'It's a male fault, isn't it? Wanting to keep the emotional stuff simple, even when it isn't and can't be.'

'I'm glad you admit it!'

'Good. Then let me explain. Irene is my—or I should say *was* my—'

'Before you go on...' Before you dig yourself in deeper, with things I know to be lies, which I wouldn't be able to bear... I think you should know that I've talked to Irene on the phone.'

'*Talked* to her? When?' he asked blankly.

She was grimly satisfied to see the way her words brought him up short.

'On Friday. When she left that message for you to ring her while you were at lunch.'

'She got me on my mobile immediately afterwards.'

'I thought she would. I suggested she try your mobile again once she'd rung off.'

'And what did she tell you?'

'Not much. Enough.'

'Then when you saw us together on Saturday...'

'It came as no surprise, only as confirmation,' she agreed tightly.

'Irene and I are *not* involved with each other, Stevie. God, *that's* not what you think, is it?'

'What I think—' an attempt at lightness '—is that my definition of involvement would probably have a lot more in common with Irene's than with yours.'

'The demands she's making on me at the moment are very difficult...'

'Oh, so it's all her fault, is it?'

'*No!* Hell, I'm by no means blameless in any of this! But, please let me tell you the whole story from the beginning. There are things that Irene *can't* have told you because there are things she refuses to believe and things she simply doesn't know!'

'Things *I* don't want to know either, Julius.' She almost had her hands over her ears.

On top of everything, what I really can't bear is to hear glib justifications from him. How they're not *really* involved, it's not *really* his fault, he's not *really* shirking his responsibilities to his children and wasn't *really* deceiving me, because, because, because, because.

I'd rather stay in ignorance of the murky details, thank you. I just know that this is over.

This last thought he read clearly in her face, and the starkness of the shock and anguish she read there gave her a terrible, twisting pang of regret and love.

He *is* hurt. I'm not the only one who's suffering.

But then she hardened her heart. He should have considered this possibility earlier. If he really wanted me, he should have had the courage to wait until his relationship with Irene was *really* over. What *is* his definition of 'not involved'? I wonder.

Not sleeping together? For how long has that been? Not living together? Not sharing a bank account? Or perhaps he's still doing all of the above, but somehow it doesn't *count* because he's just about to wriggle free. Oh, I should just have slammed the door in his face!

He was watching her helplessly now, wondering—she could read this so clearly—if it was any use trying to take her into his arms.

It wasn't. She glared at him and he understood it for himself.

'I don't see any point in prolonging this, do you?' she told him now.

'No…' He turned towards the door, and she saw with bitter relief the approaching end of this awful interview. Then he rebelled and wheeled to face her again. *'No!'* he said again, and this time it wasn't a weary agreement to her own statement. 'I won't accept this, Stevie. Hasn't it been…*isn't* it… so good between us? I hadn't thought that you could be so unforgiving. You're such a generous person.'

'Generous…and my generosity should extend to sharing you with another woman?'

'Look, she needs me. I have to—'

'I've noticed. At all hours of the day and night. At weekends. At work. And so do the children. Where does it end, Julius? With your climbing into her bed and agreeing that, after all, you can't live without each other?'

'No!'

'She wants it, Julius.'

'I know.' He nodded, and his casual acceptance twisted the knife deeper. 'But *I* don't! Can't you believe that?'

'No. I can't. I can't believe that I could win out against the full baggage of your past together, not when you're still carrying so much of it around with you. Admit it, Julius, will Irene ever really be out of your life?'

'No,' he conceded tiredly. 'She won't.'

This time he did not turn back again, and this time, when it was too late, it was Stevie who desperately wanted to start again, keep talking, find an answer. The red tail lights of his car had already disappeared down the street, but she had his mobile number. She could dial it right now and bring him back with just a few words.

Cool it, cool it, cool it, she chanted to herself. Did you

send him away on a whim? Did you really just end this on a whim?

The tangled issues sang like wires in the wind inside her head.

It's not that I couldn't deal with an ex-wife and step-children. I'm not naïve enough to think it would be easy and effortless to forge a relationship with Irene and Kyle and Lauren, but I'd have done it, put my utmost into it, *loved* the children if they let me, if they'd been there from the beginning, open and talked about, with their roles clearly defined.

A divorce which had been finalised six months ago. Or a separation which had begun last year when he'd moved into his own place.

Knowing from the beginning that he saw his children every second weekend and two nights during the week, and that I'd be bound to get involved in picking them up from Irene's and dropping them off, packing their overnight bags and ringing her to say they'd left their homework behind.

But to hear her talking about 'my partner' as if he still is, to see so clearly how much she wants him, and to know how much they see each other, when he hasn't breathed a word about her to me... It's like checking into a five-star hotel and finding that the sheets are rumpled and the bed is still warm.

I can't do it, and he was *wrong—badly* wrong—not to tell me! If this is his idea of how to conduct a relationship, then I can't forgive it. It just wouldn't work.

The burr of his mobile phone, coming from the passenger seat beside him, brought Julius out of his brooding reverie of regret. He snatched it up and pulled over to park at once, certain that it would be Stevie, summoning him back. His blood sang with relief in his veins.

'Julius?' said Irene.

How was it possible to have his spirits plummet again so fast? It left him light-headed and dizzy, as if the response was actually physical.

'Yes, Irene?'

'I'm having trouble with the computer again.'

He groaned aloud into the phone.

'I'm sorry,' she went on quickly. 'I know it's annoying.'

So annoying that, half an hour ago, on his way to Stevie's, he'd have said a cold-blooded, implacable no and slammed down the phone. Now, though, there was no reason not to accede to her demand. To *all* of her demands. In many ways, it would be so very easy to slip back into the role he had filled in her life for so long, only this time going far deeper. Easy, and as neat and rosy as a fairy tale.

But he knew he couldn't do it. 'I'll give you an hour,' he told her curtly, 'and then you're on your own.'

It was an hour—maybe a little more—after Julius's departure that the doorbell pealed again, and Stevie was so sure it would be him that she seriously considered not answering the door at all.

But that was too cowardly. Much, much too cowardly.

Instead, squaring her jaw and her shoulders and lifting her chin, she practically wrenched the thing off its hinges…then gasped at the sight of Lizzy, shaky and tearful and in pieces.

She dragged the other woman inside. 'I was about to have a gin and tonic. Like one, too?'

'Large?' said Liz.

'*Very* large. With ice and a lime wedge and a mint leaf. The works.'

'Sounds…positively medicinal.'

'It will be!'

'Why do *you* need one?' An arrowing glance, which was uncomfortably searching, shot in Stevie's direction. 'Is it because—? I mean, I've been a total pig to you since Friday, I know that.'

'It doesn't matter. Really,' Stevie said, sidestepping Liz's question. 'I think I understand.'

They went through to the kitchen and Stevie prepared the drinks while Lizzy sat at the kitchen table, still looking horribly tired and nervy.

'Oh, Stevie, I'm so scared!' she finally burst out, taking the cool, brimming drink in her shaking hand.

'You do think it must be cancer, don't you?' Stevie said, sensing that there was no need to prevaricate tonight.

'It…it has to be, doesn't it? The fatigue, the weight loss. I didn't sleep at all last night. Just terrified, Stevie. *Physically.* And I was brutal to you, when you were trying to help.'

'That's not important. You can hate me for it if you want to, but *just see a doctor*!'

'Of course I don't hate you. But…make an appointment for me?' Liz said weakly.

'At Southshore?'

'At Southshore. That one on Saturday… Dr Marr… He seemed good. Is he?'

'Yes. Very.' Tight, double-edged. Liz, fortunately, hadn't noticed.

'Him, then. Or anyone. I don't care, really.'

'They're all good.'

'I can't go on feeling this scared. You were right. Even if it's…the worst…it's far better to know.'

'It is,' Stevie agreed quietly.

Far better to know. *She* knew now, about Julius. And was that better? It had to be.

*   *   *

'Well, here I am. Wish me luck!' said Lizzy, appearing out of the blue on Wednesday at the front desk.

Stevie stared at her blankly, then pulled out of the same circular thought track she'd been stuck in for days.

Should I have listened to his rationale? Should I have accepted it? Should I have 'understood' everything and promised to go along with whatever he wanted? I'd still *have* him then, even if only in half-measure, even if it came with jealousy and loneliness and never being quite sure where I stood...

But, of course, it might still have ended somewhere down the track with me feeling like this, only with the added pain of long-time involvement, and the added sting of having *him* decide to end it. This way, at least I have my pride. My useless, comfortless pride...

'Lizzy!' she said at last. 'Your appointment!'

'Yes. It *is* today, right? You said when you rang me yesterday evening...'

'Yes, of course, I—My goodness, is it that late already?'

'Eleven. That's what you told me.'

'Yes, and Dr Marr is running right on time.' She forced the appropriate briskness and good cheer into her tone. 'So I'd better run your card through the machine and get you to fill out this form.'

'It's a lovely, bright atmosphere,' Lizzy said as she got out her card. 'I'd thought a health centre would be shabby and crowded and noisy, but it's not, is it?' She sounded a little jittery, as she had on Monday night. *Very* jittery. Still scared.

It was good, working here. You couldn't be allowed to forget that other people had problems too. Things snapped back into perspective just a little for Stevie. Poor Liz was facing a cancer scare...

'Try and think carefully about what you put on the form,'

she told her friend gently. 'The more accuracy and detail you use, the easier it will be for Dr Marr to rule out one problem or pinpoint another.'

'OK.' Liz nodded.

She was such a capable-looking person, big-boned and starting to grey, with wide cheek-bones and dark, sooty eyes. She'd had many men interested in her since her divorce from Pete, but she didn't seem to be looking for another marriage and she wasn't involved with anyone at the moment.

If this *was* cancer or something equally serious, she'd have to face it, in many ways, alone, and her Amazonian stature would count for nothing then.

A few minutes later, she put the completed form on the front desk, but Stevie was on the phone and could only smile at her. Then, before Liz even sat down again, Julius appeared to call her in, wearing a white coat thrown casually over his dark grey patterned shirt.

'No, Friday afternoon's no good,' said the anonymous patient at the far end of the phone. 'How about Thursday afternoon?'

'Well, Dr Irwin doesn't come in on Thursdays at the moment...' Stevie explained mechanically, watching Julius stand back to let Lizzy through. The latter went, with the air of wondering whether she'd ever return. Stevie had not asked Julius to give special attention to her friend. She didn't need to. Julius Marr was scrupulously attentive and thorough with everyone.

Stevie found it harder to be as scrupulously attentive to her own work. As well as the demands of the phone lines and patients in person at the desk, Aimee Hilliard had just breezed in with a very satisfied look on her lightly tanned face.

At fifty, she was a trim and attractive woman, with the

sort of classic bone structure and Nordic blue eyes that were agelessly lovely, and today there was an added splash of colour in her cheeks.

'Well, I got it!' she announced in a satisfied tone.

'The job at Dr Irwin's practice?' squeaked Cathy Hong. '*Fabulous*, Aimee! Wasn't that the one you most wanted?'

'Did I say that?' Her smile was a little vague, and the two spots of colour grew a little brighter. 'Actually, yes...' She buried her face in the vase of fresh flowers on the reception desk, as if to drink in their scent, and said with her face in shadow, 'It *did* have some definite advantages. Not too far from home. A smaller practice than this one, which I think I'll like. I start the week after next, which fits perfectly with finishing here next Friday.'

'And, of course, you know Rebecca Irwin from her hours here.'

'She was the one who told me they were looking for someone.' Aimee nodded.

'She's in practice with her father and her fiancé and one other woman, isn't she?' Cathy asked.

'Yes, and they all seem nice. Grace Gaines was the only one I hadn't met before. And I must say Rebecca's Dr Jones is a good-looking piece of manhood!'

But he's not the one she's attracted to, Stevie thought, the flash of perception surprising her. My emotions are running so deep at the moment, it's as if I'm seeing and sharing what everyone else is feeling twice as strongly as I normally would.

Aimee's attracted to Rebecca Irwin's father, the man she's going to be working for, but she doesn't want to admit it, even to herself. Sally Kitchin is struggling to keep her head above water with those three babies. And Liz is terrified of cancer.

Only when Liz came out of Dr Marr's office ten minutes

later she wasn't terrified any more. She was a whole new woman, and she grinned as she came up to Stevie at the desk.

'He doesn't think it's cancer at all. He thinks it's almost certainly my thyroid, and I remember now that Mum had problems with hers in her forties. She had to have radiation treatment to shrink it, but that did the trick and she's been fine ever since. She never mentions it, which is why I didn't even *think*— Oh, Stevie, thank you so much for forcing the issue and making me come in, and saving me from weeks of worry and fear! You were right. It *is* always best to know!'

'It is,' Steve agreed firmly, though there was a part of her which couldn't help wondering, in her own case, if the opposite was true.

For her, ignorance had been bliss, and her fool's paradise a much nicer place to inhabit than this cold little island landscaped only with the solid rock of her certainty that she'd acted with strength and honour.

She hid all this from Lizzy, of course, and said only, 'If you need help with anything, please, ask, and if you have any questions about the treatment don't hesitate to ring Dr Marr. He's always willing to take time over the phone and he hates to find out that a patient has been left confused or uncertain.

'I could see that,' Liz said. 'I understand now why he was such a help to you and your mum. He's a real find.'

And she was too full of relief to notice the ambivalence of Stevie's agreement.

That night, Stevie planned to make her promised visit to Sally Kitchin, but in the event the timing was wrong, and she received some very convincing evidence that it wasn't necessary. Going out to the clothesline at six to take down the laundry she had hung up that morning, she stumbled upon a delightful spectacle.

Most of the Kitchins' lawn was sadly in need of mowing, but one patch, circle-shaped, was freshly cut, as was a stripe that led to the house, making a path. In the middle of the circle stood a table, and on it, keeping the gathering dusk at bay, were three long and elegant candles, two blue and one pink, their light flickering against a white cloth.

It was a mild evening, and there sat Sally and her husband, Michael, with take-away pizza slices set on elegant china, a bag of salad greens from the supermarket, newly decanted into a glass salad bowl, and a gourmet cheesecake in a clear plastic box awaiting their attention later on. A tall bottle of wine sat between them, as well as a slightly less tall baby monitor, emitting the snuffling sounds and amplified creaks and rustlings of three babies safely asleep in their nursery.

Both Sally and Michael had eyes only for each other—until Stevie's 'Hills Hoist' rotary clothesline creaked as she removed a sheet and it caught their attention. They came over to the fence, both beaming.

'He's got his promotion and a much bigger salary, and he's here, and he doesn't have to go away again for at least six months!' Sally said. 'And he's got three weeks off, starting Friday—'

'And I'm going to *make* her sleep in every single day of it!' Michael said firmly, with another grin. '*And* take an afternoon nap! It's about time I had the chance to get to know my three beautiful children!'

Sally was in tears and laughing at the same time. 'Oh, Stevie,' she said, 'I was a mess at the health centre last week, wasn't I?'

'Dr Marr was afraid you might be suffering from postnatal depression,' Stevie acknowledged, feeling it was safe to do so.

'Looking back, I'm not surprised,' Sally admitted. 'I was close to the end of the rope. Just exhausted, really, as I know I'll be again. I'm also on cloud nine a lot of the time. Like today. And when they smile. And when they're asleep all at once! And when I smell their hair…'

'Hair? I haven't seen any hair!' Michael protested.

'Oh, they *do* have hair!' Sally insisted. 'I mean, fuzz… That's hair. In the right light,' she admitted sheepishly. 'OK, so it's my maternal delusion. They *haven't* got hair, but their *heads* still smell fabulous, and they're holding them up so beautifully now.'

A few minutes later Stevie finished taking in her washing and left the Kitchins to their candle-lit pizza for two.

'Sally's idea, but I mowed the lawn,' Michael had said, and Stevie knew that a mother who could carry out a quirky yet very romantic celebration like this could not be in the grips of true postnatal depression.

She told Julius so the next day, taking the easy way out and grabbing him on his way through Reception so that there were other people about.

He appeared pleased at her report on Sally, and agreed with her perception about Sally's state.

'Still,' he added, 'I'll drop in and see her myself in a week or two. I'm…wary of miracles, I suppose.'

'Wary?' she echoed carefully.

Where was he taking this? Ros was well within earshot. Could she possibly miss the undertone of meaning that Stevie had heard so clearly?

'In my experience,' he said, 'there are no easy answers, and anything that's worthwhile demands hard work. I hate to declare prematurely that the race is won, and I also hate to declare that it's lost,' he finished.

Stevie flashed an emotion-filled glance at him, then dropped her gaze to stare down at her fingers. He means us, she thought. He's telling me I gave up too soon.

Aware of the growing silence between them, she hesitated. A few words from her, and he would ask her out again, ask if they could have another try, talk things over, work to reach an understanding.

But she hardened her heart once more. He's putting this onto me, she realised. Making it into *my* fault. Well, it's *not* my fault! I wasn't wrong to expect honesty from him!

Lifting her head, she said very clearly, 'I don't agree. There are times when it's only wrong and foolish to go on trying. You have to trust what you feel, put your mistakes behind you and move on.'

'That's what you believe?'

'Yes.'

'Very well, then.' He gave a curt nod, flung a brief word to anyone who was listening and disappeared into his office.

'What was *that* about?' Ros wanted to know.

'Just a patient,' Stevie answered. It was half-true, anyway.

'Is that all?'

'Er…more or less.'

'Because I'm worried about that man,' Ros went on.

'Are you?'

'Stevie, he looks as if he's being stretched on the rack! Something is hurting him very badly, and on top of all that fatigue and preoccupation I've seen in him for the past few months. I hope he isn't heading for a breakdown!'

'A breakdown! Surely that's melodramatic?'

'People have them. Even doctors have them.'

'But still…'

'Stevie, he's at the end of his tether, and if I knew who was doing this to him, I'd really tell them where to get off!'

The strength drained from Stevie's legs. It was true. He *was* miserable. She'd seen it often enough over the past few days but had considered it as a reflection of her own emotion and had felt a bitter satisfaction that he was feeling as bad as she was. Now her heart lurched with remorse.

Does he really love me, then, as much as I love him? Does that mean he's right? That I'm wrong to give up? That I should work harder to understand and forgive?

The two ways of thinking warred inside her—on the one hand, her innate instinct to trust and understand, and on the other her fear of being naïve and her awareness of her own vulnerability. So many men made selfish capital out of a woman's need to trust.

Still, though, Ros's words had had an effect, and Stevie got through her week and her weekend with just a little less pain and a little more hope.

CHAPTER EIGHT

JULIUS blinked at the clock, a movement which sent sharp pain radiating outwards across the tight muscles of his head.

Two in the morning, and he was still at his desk, struggling over the wording of his description of a crucial phase in his research.

'The control group contained,' he wrote, then scribbled out the last word.

He should be entering this straight onto the computer, but his head might very possibly explode if he had to look for another minute at a bright screen.

'The control group consisted of,' he amended, 'fifteen children at the upper end of the—'

No, that was needlessly wordy. Again, he crossed out the last few words. His style normally flowed along much better than this.

He laid his head down on the desk for a moment. Just a minute to relax and close his eyes. He had made up his mind he wouldn't stop before three, and had already set the alarm for eight in the morning. A Sunday sleep-in, of sorts. If he could just keep up this pace for another month, then the work would be done.

And then, only then, would he try again to talk to Stevie, to make promises to her that he knew he'd be able to keep, and to tell her, if she'd let him, every nuance in his long and complex and necessary relationship with Irene.

It felt like a good resolution.

I won't go to Stevie with my double life still wreaking

havoc between us. I'll get it resolved. That's why I *must* work now. I must get this *done*!

It immediately became a more important motivation than all the submission deadlines of all the medical journals in the world.

I must...take just one more minute, and then I must...lift...my...head...

Seconds later he was asleep, and when he awoke it was four, his whole body was aching as well as his head and he knew that the only sensible thing to do was to crawl straight into bed. Absolutely the only sensible thing to do. Instead, he rose stiffly, got two headache pills from his bathroom cabinet, made coffee and resumed work.

'Fifteen children aged between ten and twelve years, with a family history of...'

He completed the handwritten draft of his paper just as dawn struck the cream-painted brick of the east wall of his terrace house.

'I'm sorry to do this to you,' said Aimee Hilliard to Stevie at five o'clock on Tuesday.

'No,' she urged in reply. 'You look terrible. You must go home.'

'But you weren't supposed to be working late at all to-night, and now you'll be the last to leave. If Cathy didn't have to go out, she, at least, could have done my job while you staffed the front desk and got to leave a bit earlier.'

'It's fine, really,' Stevie urged again.

Aimee was coming down with flu and clearly needed to pack herself off to bed with a ready supply of hot liquids, but she was concerned about leaving her role in tonight's heart health class for Stevie to play.

Stevie had her own qualms. Aimee was a fully qualified nurse. How would young, energetic Dr McKinnon feel about having only an untrained receptionist with an ancient memory of her year of nursing as his substitute assistant tonight?

But if she thinks I'm nervous she won't go home, so I can't let her see it. She's a mess, and she looks feverish.

'Go, Aimee. I'll grab dinner somewhere down the road and be ready for Dr McKinnon by seven-thirty, don't you worry.'

'Seven-fifteen,' Aimee corrected at once. 'He'll have some setting up for you to do.'

'Seven-fifteen, then,' Stevie promised, and at last Aimee, visibly aching, was persuaded to depart in her pert little car.

There was a flood of patients between five-thirty and six, but Cathy, who was eating out late tonight, had brought her own snack and Stevie was thus able to walk down to a noodle house on Anzac Parade at a quarter to seven and get a steaming container full of Singapore rice noodles and prawns.

She ate it on the hop in the meetings room as she shuttled about, setting the place up according to Dr McKinnon's not very explicit instructions.

Of all the seven doctors at the centre, Cameron McKinnon was the one she felt least relaxed with. It was her own fault, she was sure, as he had a good reputation with the rest of the staff, but he was just so…so *young*, and so keen, and so clever.

All the doctors were clever, of course… Julius was perhaps the cleverest, since you didn't spend years in medical research without a considerable quantity of good brain. But somehow the others didn't *show* it as Dr McKinnon did.

Or perhaps intelligence wore itself better in those who were over thirty. Dr McKinnon, who'd graduated from high school with outstanding results at just sixteen years of age, was still only twenty-six.

'You see what a fantastic machine the human body is,' he was saying to his mixed group of listeners at five past nine. 'But let's treat it right. Let's give it the right fuel and drive it at the right speed, and really make our engines *purr*!'

He was charismatic, no doubt about that, and so energetic that he'd single-handedly managed most of the nursing tasks usually handled by Aimee at these sessions, such as taking the blood pressure and pulse of several people at rest and after exercise in order to illustrate some points on fitness.

Stevie, left just to hand out fact sheets, collect up models of the heart and perform other such tasks, had felt distinctly superfluous at times.

Now, though, as the session finished, Dr McKinnon handed all the work back to her. 'I have to go straight away,' he said cheerfully. 'Can you pack up and lock the place?'

'Of course. If you'll just tell me where—'

But he had already gone, after flinging a casual word of thanks back over his shoulder and not even hearing her words.

Stevie shrugged. No problem. She'd locked up here before. She waited as everyone picked up their bags and jackets and filed out, then locked the door behind them and set about clearing away tea-and coffee-cups, stacking chairs and returning unused class materials to the cupboard in the corner of the room.

She didn't feel the slightest bit nervous about being alone—after all, she'd been living alone now for several months—until she heard the noise of footsteps out in the corridor that led from the back entrance to the main reception area.

She froze. Had the back door been locked? Through which door had Cameron McKinnon made his breezy exit?

I won't be an idiot. I'll see who it is before I panic.

She walked…no, she *crept*…up to the door and peered out, just as someone rounded the corner.

Julius.

The relief must have shown in her face.

'You're still here?' he said, coming up to her. It was the closest—and the most *alone*—they'd been together since Monday's catastrophic scene, over a week ago now.

His nearness…and his eagerness…was painfully sweet and hard to bear. She had to struggle against her overwhelming awareness in order to speak.

'Just locking up,' she said. 'You startled me, actually.'

'I came to get some notes I'd forgotten,' he explained. 'I've chucked them in my desk somewhere and it'll probably take me a few minutes to find them. Want me to lock up?'

'No, because I still have the cups to wash and half the chairs to stack.'

'Who left you with all of this?' he demanded.

'It's fine,' she insisted. 'Everyone was strapped today, and everyone had a reason to leave early.'

'I'll help you, then.'

'I don't mind doing it. You look for your notes… Please!'

It was this last word that convinced him. Without that he might have insisted, but it had come out with a weak sort of desperation that betrayed how hard it was for her to be with him like this. He'd stiffened now.

'Of course. OK.'

'I'll just…' she muttered meaninglessly, and fled.

Ten minutes of work put everything in order, and though she hadn't heard his movements again she assumed he must have left. His desk was untidy, but not so untidy that it could take him that long to locate notes which he must have been working on only recently.

She went out into the reception area with the big bunch of health-centre keys in her hand and then glanced around one last time to check that everything was in order. It was. Good! She flicked the three switches that controlled the remaining lights and now the place was in darkness apart from one light immediately above the nearest exit door.

Hang on, though. Not quite in darkness. A faint golden sheen stretched down the corridor from the direction of several of the offices. She sighed, knowing she had better investigate. Someone had evidently left a light on at the end of evening appointments.

It wasn't until she got quite close that she realised the light was coming from under Julius's door. There was also a strange, rhythmic sound... Was he still in there, then?

She knocked softly and waited. No response. And when she carefully opened the door she realised why. With his head dropped onto his desk, as if the pile of papers there were a soft feather pillow, and arms flung in front of him, Julius was asleep.

That rhythmic sound had been his breathing—Stevie was generous enough not to call it snoring—and it didn't change as she tiptoed in and laid a hand on his shoulder.

'Wake up, Julius. You can't do this. You'll feel *terrible* in the morning!'

'Who?' He stirred and sat up groggily, one cheek marked red by the edge of the heap of papers.

Realising what had happened, he made a disgusted sound and covered his face with his capable hands. Gorgeous hands. Hands that had caressed her intimately just two weeks ago.

Stevie's heart turned over. He looked, as Ros had said the other day, close to breaking down. 'You'd better let me drive you home,' she said.

'No. I'll wake up in a minute.' He slapped his cheeks with his palms, but his eyes still held that over-brightness which meant that fatigue was deep and total.

'Why are you driving yourself like this?' she demanded, hating the fact that she cared so much. All she wanted to do was go up to him and pull him against her, as if her own comparative strength and energy could travel into him and give him what he needed to go on.

She hadn't really expected an answer to her wild question, but he gave one at once, wearily and with a pale smile. 'Because of you, Stevie.'

'Me?' She gave a tight laugh. 'What's that supposed to mean?'

'If I can complete my commitment to this research—damn it, I don't want to say this to you now—then when I ask you again to be my lover, I'll have the time to give you what you deserve. I'll be able to put you first in my life, Stevie, and I was wrong, before, to try and have you when I couldn't give you that.'

'Oh, God,' she whispered. 'Have I been that demanding? That selfish?'

Unconsciously, she moved towards him.

'No, of course you haven't. At least— You had every right to feel ill-used, and I *will* make it up to you. Another month, that's all. Six weeks at the most. Another paper to write, and one to revise.'

'And if you try to do that in a month, as well as everything you have to do here, you'll break down from exhaustion, Julius. Don't do it. Take the time you need. You don't need to wait for me. I—I'm here now. I'll be and do whatever you need *now*, Julius. I don't want to make you wreck yourself for me.'

She was so concerned for him, so full of love, and his words were so heartfelt that she forgot that it was Irene, and not his work, that she resented. Irene who had broken them apart, not the long hours he spent moulding data into coherent conclusions.

She had reached him now and put her hands out to run them across his fatigue-bowed shoulders, and bent to bury her face in his thick, fragrant hair. Having fought the need to do this for eleven long days, she now gave into it completely, almost trembling with the fulfilment of touching him again.

He shuddered and swivelled in his chair to pull her down to him, taking her onto his lap and winding his arms around her. Eyes closed against the tears that burned in them, Stevie quested hungrily and helplessly for his mouth, and when she found it she let his kiss wash over her, fill her and drown out all other awareness.

All she knew was the slight roughness of his skin, the warmth of his breath on her face, the taste of him…

His arms loosened around her now and his hand came to brush against her breasts, fondling their firm, petite shape so that they strained and tightened and tingled inside the satin cups of her bra.

She trembled with the need aroused in her by his touch and reached out again to caress his face as she kissed it— those dark brows, the long planes of his cheeks, his wide, square jaw. This face, which was already so impossibly precious to her…

Pressing her lips against his forehead, as if the heat of her mouth could iron away the pleats of fatigue imprinted there, she could still taste him—a deliciously rich, slightly bitter and almost smoky flavour. He must have drunk a lot of coffee today. Perhaps, in fact, he'd taken in nothing but.

Still holding his face, she asked with gentle accusation, 'Did you eat tonight?'

'Not yet.'

'And just when were you planning to?'

'Oh…' He shrugged vaguely. 'There's something I can put in the microwave when I get home, I think.'

'Don't. Let me cook for you. Come home to my place. I've got plenty in the fridge.'

But his answer was decisive. 'No. Make it my place.'

'Because of your work?'

'No, Stevie.' He looked at her. 'Because I want you to see where I live. If you're going to insist on being em-broiled in this complicated life of mine, I want to have you on my own turf for once. Somehow, the fact that we always ended up at your place before made your exclusion seem more extreme. It's something else I regret. I just didn't want you to see…' he gave a disarming smile '…what it looks like on the days when my housekeeper doesn't come.'

'But she's been today?' Stevie teased.

'I certainly hope so!'

'I love you, Julius,' she said.

The words just came out. I love you. Spoken on a tender laugh because the idea of him being a little helpless around the house and so fervently dependent on his housekeeper somehow held enormous appeal. Saying them, that had not been planned, and she was appalled at the weight they seemed to make in the air.

I love you. Just words. But such powerful ones. She felt him freeze, then gradually relax. Movement returned to his body, like warmth returning to chilled skin.

'I love you, too, Stevie,' he said carefully.

'I'm sorry,' she blurted.

'Why?'

'Because…because saying it like that made you say it.'

'I didn't have to say it,' he pointed out gently.

'But if you hadn't… I mean, when one person does, then the other person is almost *obliged*…'

He put two fingers across her mouth to silence her. 'They're just words, Stevie.'

The fingers slowly caressed the fullness of her bottom lip, then outlined the bow of her upper one. Finally he replaced the fingers with his mouth, giving her no time to decide whether what he had said, the echo of her own thought, had been meant as reassurance or dismissal. If a kiss could communicate love, though…

She sighed raggedly and lost herself once more in the magic of his mouth until the moment of awkwardness was forgotten.

What could not be forgotten for long, however, was the fact that he was hungry. His stomach rumbled to announce the fact and they both laughed.

'You never said,' he pointed out tenderly. 'Would you like to come back to my place?'

'I'd love to,' she whispered.

Abandoning her own car in the health-centre car park without a second thought, she cocooned herself happily in the passenger seat of his as he had rejected her insistence that he was too tired to take the wheel. There was a stiff sea breeze tonight and her thinly stockinged legs were chilled below the calf-length hem of her rust-red dress.

It was after nine-thirty now, and the drive to Surry Hills along Anzac Parade did not take long. Soon he was turning off into Cleveland Street and thence to a side street of lovingly restored Victorian terraces, most with their elaborate iron lace intact and many revealing dramatic extensions at the back which added light and space to what had originally been quite humble dwellings.

Julius's house was just such a place, with a study opening off the front passage and then a living room, dining room and state-of-the-art kitchen, all looking out onto a conservatory and courtyard which would make the transition between interior and exterior completely seamless on a sunny day.

The place was gorgeous…

'Your housekeeper hasn't let you down,' Stevie said.

Yet it was oddly sparse in its furnishings. The basics were there, particularly in the study, although she'd taken one look at the clutter of papers and jumble of computer equipment in that room and had refrained from a closer examination.

But where were the details? Lounge suite, coffee table, television and audio equipment, yes, but no bookshelves, end tables or reading lamps and only one picture on the cream-painted walls. This, though, was clearly an original oil, showing a market stall with fruit and vegetables, painted in bold, sensuous colour, and she loved it on sight.

The dining room, when she followed him through it, was the same—table and set of eight chairs, very new-looking, and a gorgeous pair of pale green oriental vases on the beautifully preserved mantelpiece above the marble fireplace, and nothing else in the room at all.

'I haven't been living here very long,' he said, 'which explains what you might have noticed…'

'Yes…'

'That I don't have quite enough *stuff* to fill it.'

'It is a little spartan in places,' she had to agree.

He made a face. 'You should have seen it a few months ago, before I got the dining set.'

'Well, it's a mistake to rush into buying a lot of things at once,' she answered evenly, disguising her thought track.

It's because of Irene and their split, she thought. He's been turfed out of the conjugal home and given custody of the sound system, the computer and the painting. And maybe he's stalled on filling the gaps because he's still been hoping they'd get back together.

Oh, God, am I a fool to be here? Nothing's changed! Irene is still a huge element in his life, and the children. I wonder what it's like upstairs? Are there beds for them? Does he have them on weekends?

I *can* deal with it. Plenty of women have to. Am I being horribly ungenerous? We're so good together... I love him so much... It's unreasonable of me to expect perfection in a relationship. Julius is the honey, and his past with Irene, still impinging so much on his life now, is the sting in the tail.

If I'm getting involved again...and I am, oh, God, I know I am...then I *must* ask him for more. He tried to tell me before and I wouldn't listen. This time I have to listen. I have to know how matters stand. At least this proves it really is over. He's not living with her.

Only I can't ask now...tonight...God, *look* at him!

He had moved ahead into the kitchen and was prowling there aimlessly, opening cupboards and looking into the fridge, clearly not having a clue about how to get himself a decent meal at this hour in his state of weariness. He was far too tired and hungry to notice her own well-concealed difficulties.

Her heart turned over and she pushed all thoughts of Irene aside. She was here with him now, wasn't she? And he'd said, just half an hour ago, that he loved her. What more did she want?

'There's all sorts of stuff,' he said. 'When I know I'm

going to be home I get her to cook for me sometimes, and she buys things.' It took Stevie a long, painful moment to realise he was talking about his housekeeper, not about Irene. 'Hell, I'm starving, but what can we cook up at this hour?'

'*We* can't cook up anything. But *I'll* make something,' she told him. 'Relax, Julius. Just sit and relax while I do it. Have a drink or…a bath, or something.'

'A bath?' He gave a shout of laughter. 'I haven't even used the bath in this place, although I've been here over six months. Mrs Ferguson polishes it beautifully every week, too. Do you know, the idea appeals…?'

'Do it, then,' she insisted softly. 'Let me cook. I like it.'

He did not protest further, just took a stride towards her and enfolded her once more in his arms.

'Do I deserve you, I wonder…?' he muttered, then covered Stevie's mouth in a kiss that almost seemed to contain doubt. It was incongruous in such an utterly imposing, utterly successful man. Moved at even this small hint of vulnerability, she kissed him with her love trembling there on her lips.

'Come and wake me up when dinner's ready?' he suggested finally.

'Wake you up? I thought you were having a bath!'

'I am. But I'll probably go to sleep in it.'

She didn't believe him.

Half an hour later, however, when a thick steak was ready to be laid on his heated plate, two large microwave-baked potatoes already sat there, steaming as they clamoured for their butter. Nearby was a tossed salad filled with avocado, tomato, marinated artichokes and olives, as well as oak-leaf lettuce awaited its dressing. She went upstairs, found the bathroom and saw that he hadn't been exaggerating.

For the second time that day she found Julius asleep, and this time the sight was so beautiful—that long, male body sprawled in the water, those wide shoulders nestled in the curve of the white porcelain, his smooth mouth softly closed and his lashes resting against his cheeks—that she could only creep forward and sit on the edge of the tub, watching him for a full minute before reaching out to brush his bare collar-bone with the backs of her fingers.

He didn't wake. She let her hand drift further, up to his jaw and into his hair, then down again, to his shoulder, to his chest where just the right amount of dark hair made a symmetrical pattern, then lower, into the now-tepid water...

He stirred, opened his eyes and smiled. 'I did, didn't I?' he said.

'Like a log,' she agreed, understanding at once. 'But your meal's ready now, and it's steak so—'

'Steak!' His eyes lit up, and his tone was awed.

She laughed and left him to dress while she went down to put it on his plate and add the dressing to the salad.

Five minutes later he was eating hungrily while she watched him. She was sipping the glass of red wine he'd urged on her, saying 'I won't eat a huge, fabulous meal like this while you have *nothing*!'

It was a good sight, this, watching the man she loved as he ate, a very immediate and surprisingly sensual pleasure—the way his mouth moved, the way he kept smiling his appreciation at her, the way his hands looked as he lifted his glass in a silent toast to her kitchen skills.

I won't think of anything else, she decided. I won't poison this with doubt. We're here together. That's what counts.

And it counted later, too, when he'd finished the full plate and had flung the dishes unceremoniously into the sink. They didn't need to talk about what was happening next. Somehow it was as obvious as summer following spring.

His bed. Together. Not a crazy, feverish joining of their bodies, because they were both too weary for that now, but a more gentle, unambitious love-making, full of soft, lazy, sleepy caresses that segued gradually into an effortless joining.

There was nothing lazy about their shared climax, however. She gasped when it came, ambushed by its intensity when she still felt so deliciously relaxed, then moaned aloud in chorus with his own triumphant cries of release until they were still again.

Predictably, he fell asleep first, and she took greedy advantage of the fact, cherishing the weight of his head on her arm, the relaxed cup of his hand around her breast, the sheer, warm, glorious mass of him lolled against her length to length, and lay there for a long time not wanting sleep to come at all.

Finally, though, she felt drowsiness overtaking her as inevitably as a tide, and her last conscious thought was, Morning will come too soon. I know it...

It came sooner even than she had feared, and much more jarring and horrible.

That sound, jangling with rhythmic insistence so close to her ear... Was it a particularly obnoxious alarm? But surely it was still pitch dark! Surely it wasn't morning yet!

She struggled into wakefulness and realised that it was the phone on the small table by her side of the bed. Beside it sat a clock-radio alarm, and the time read three a.m. The intrusive sound was only just beginning to drag Julius from his deep sleep, she noticed.

Oh, stop, you horrible thing! Who could be ringing at this hour?

Her only thought being to silence the maddening insistence of it, she picked the phone up, prepared for a wrong number, prepared for an overseas caller who had calculated the time difference wrongly, prepared for anything except what she heard after her own creaky, 'Hello?'

A distraught woman's voice barked a loud, uncontrolled, 'My God, *Julius*? No! Where's Julius? Who *is* this?'

CHAPTER NINE

SILENTLY Stevie took the phone from her ear and handed it to Julius, who was awake now and already sitting up, straight-backed and alert.

'Yes?' he said abruptly, then added, the muscles in his face drawn and tight, 'My God, Irene, what is it?'

Irene.

Stevie had known it already, of course. Even in her groggy state, and even with the woman's voice distorted by panic, she had recognised her.

But knowing and hearing the name spoken in Julius's deliciously burred voice were two different things. All the worst feelings in this very worst hour of the night ambushed Stevie and brought nausea boiling into her stomach.

She had to clench her jaw to keep it back and, with the coiled phone cord stretching across her body and the receiver still just inches from her ear, she couldn't help overhearing Irene's first high-pitched words.

'I don't want this divorce! I don't want to be alone like this!'

'Calm down, calm down. What have you been doing to yourself? What's going on?' Julius demanded at once, and now Irene must have lowered her voice a little as Stevie could no longer hear.

Misery and dismay lay like vinegar in her stomach now, and she rolled over, away from Julius, hunching herself around her pain so that she lay like a sack of potatoes in the wide bed.

How can any relationship work when it starts like this?

she asked herself. To lie in bed with him after we've made love the way we did and hear him talking on the phone to the woman he used to love…the mother of his children.

It was almost as if Irene had invited herself into bed with them, to make a perverted threesome.

Stevie didn't want to hear the conversation, which was still going on in long bursts of silence, which indicated that Irene was talking, and terse comments and questions from Julius.

She hunched lower in the bed, pulling the padded quilt up to cover her ears and pressing her hands there to drown the sound of his voice and his pauses, hoping he would think—most unlikely—that she had fallen asleep once more.

Her action did successfully block all sound, and she lay in a limbo of knotted muscles and knotted emotions until a minute later she felt him shaking her gently.

'Stevie? Stevie, are you asleep?'

'No.' She pulled the quilt down from her ears.

'I have to go.'

'Of course.' She couldn't quite keep the bite out of her voice.

Irene called him and he went, whether it was to his daughter's school fête on a Saturday afternoon or to Irene's bedroom at three in the morning.

But if he noticed her bitterness he dismissed it. 'She's threatening suicide.'

'Oh, no! That's—'

'And she's been drinking.'

'Oh, Julius, I—!'

'Look, from experience I'm certain it won't be as bad as it sounds. Stay here. Sleep out the rest of the night. If I'm not back by morning, take a taxi to work. I'll pay for it, of course.'

But she would have none of this. 'Here? How can I stay *here*? I'll get a taxi now!'

She spoke with such urgency that he didn't question her reasons. She wasn't even sure what they were herself, only that there was something obscene about this situation and she wasn't going to compound it by waiting here for him, loving him and wanting him and, yes, *hating* Irene, even while feeling painfully for her and while Julius patched together his ex-partner's reasons for living.

He did question her decision, though. 'I'm not letting you get a taxi at this hour of the morning! It isn't safe.'

'I'm *not* staying here.'

'Then I'll have to drive you home. Dress as quickly as you can, won't you? I am pretty concerned. This isn't the way she needs to deal with what's going on in her life. I know it's only a gesture, but if she misjudges it…'

He was already dressing rapidly himself, turning to his walk-in wardrobe and pulling out close-fitting navy sweatpants, a white T-shirt and a matching navy and white sweatshirt. She'd never seen him quite so casually garbed before. Dressed for action?

She could only follow his example, and wished she had something better to put on than yesterday's rust-red autumn-weight dress with its matching leather shoes and silk slip.

He was ready before she was, of course, and as she fumbled with her zip he strode from the room. She heard his voice a minute later, peremptory, cajoling and tender in the space of three short phrases, and hurried after the sound. What was he saying to her?

But it was Irene he was talking to. He had his little black mobile pressed to his ear and was on his way downstairs, speaking into it all the time as if the phone was a lifeline…which it was, Stevie realised. Irene's lifeline.

Behind him, stumbling on the stairs as she strained to catch up, she said curtly, 'You can't waste time driving me home. I won't let you!'

'And *I* won't let you take a taxi home to an empty house at three in the morning.' He turned to her impatiently, his palm over the mouthpiece of the phone. 'So what's the alternative?'

'Take me with you.' It was scarcely what she wanted, but apparently the only possible compromise.

I'm going to have to deal with Irene sooner or later, she realised. She's not going to go away! So I may as well start now.

She didn't, under the circumstances, stop to consider what a momentous decision it was. That it meant she had accepted Julius in her life with all the difficult and painful baggage of his past, and would take what the relationship dished out to her—stepchildren, a jealous ex-wife, half a lifetime of complex human dealings.

'Take you?' he said briefly, his eyes narrowed and his palm over the mouthpiece of the phone. 'Are you sure?'

'Perhaps I can help in some way,' she suggested, making it sound more simple than it felt.

He nodded, convinced, as they gained the street, then turned his attention immediately to Irene at the other end of the phone, while pulling his keys from his pocket.

At this hour of the night...or morning...they reached Rose Bay in just ten minutes. Julius and Stevie had not spoken during the journey. He'd stayed on the phone the whole time, his attention relentlessly pinned to Irene and his words to her still filled with that telling mix of anger, authority and tenderness.

At last, he said to her, 'I'm putting down the phone, OK? I'm turning into your street. *Don't move!*'

Thirty seconds later he pulled up in the driveway of a

magnificent house which surely had to have impressive views to the harbour on one side and the ocean on the other.

Irene must have brought money to the marriage, Stevie realised, because even the best medical researchers didn't earn the sort of income that would buy this. If a divorce settlement forced its sale, it would probably bring several million dollars.

Julius was impervious to the splendour, however. He had already pulled himself from the car and was starting up the curved brick walk to the flight of steps which led up to the house. Stevie followed him and watched without surprise as he fitted a key from his own keyring into the lock of the panelled front door.

Once inside his movements were just as sure, and he followed the trail of lights up a curved marble staircase to the top floor and on into a sybaritic boudoir of a bedroom.

There stood Irene, facing the doorway. She had heard their entry and was waiting for them.

'You've brought—' she began.

'Stevie' Julius nodded. 'If the children wake up...'

It was true. If the children woke up, Stevie would be there to reassure them while Julius gave Irene what she needed, though neither he nor Stevie herself had discussed this advantage to her presence until now.

Irene said nothing, but began to sob wildly as she stumbled forward. Stevie saw that she had a drink in her hand and a bottle of pale pills clutched with white-knuckled firmness in the other.

Julius saw them, too. 'Irene,' he rasped. 'You promised. You promised you wouldn't...'

But her sobs only increased and she pulled him towards the bathroom and gestured mutely at the disarray displayed there.

Stevie, standing back, could see the whole thing through

the open door—a room of luxurious opulence with bright lighting, gold-plated fittings, huge mirrors, antique furnishings and a huge Jacuzzi.

The medicine chest was gaping open, however, and pills were spilled and scattered everywhere. There was also a razor balanced on the edge of the handbasin, with a little trickle of blood threading from it towards the plug-hole.

Stevie gasped at this last detail and her stomach churned. The chaos and despair amidst the luxury made her taste guilt in her mouth like a bitter fruit.

Is it my relationship with Julius that has brought her to the edge like this? But I didn't know! He'd been living on his own for months before we got involved. And what, I wonder, has he been keeping from *her*?

The blonde woman, looking her forty years at close range, lunged crookedly towards the basin, as if to grab the razor or perhaps a handful of the scattered pills, and Stevie's heart went out to her. Julius, though, was angry now.

'I thought so!' he rasped. 'How many of these have you actually taken, Irene? What have you actually *done*?'

'I—I don't know. A few. I would have taken more, only I spilled them. My hands were shaking. That's why I couldn't use the razor.'

Her voice cracked, but Julius only swept on in an impatient tone. 'Don't give me that! I don't know what your object is, Irene, but it's not going to work. Can't you get that into your head? I don't respond to theatrics. I've learned the hard way that it doesn't pay, with you, and if you haven't realised that by now, then…' He didn't bother to finish. 'Now, do you have any syrup of ipecac here?'

He didn't wait for an answer, but began to dig through the impressive array of medicines, salves and potions in the gaping cabinet. He soon found what he wanted.

'What are you doing?' Irene asked harshly.

'If you're going to behave like a child, I'll treat you like one. I'm going to give you a good dose of this, and if by some slender chance you *have* taken enough of these artistically arranged goodies to risk damaging yourself you'll bring them all up again before they can do you any harm. There's no spoon in here. Stevie, go down to the kitchen and bring one, would you? And a glass of watered-down juice to take the taste away once the business is over with?'

'Where…?'

'You'll find the kitchen at the end of the passage behind the stairs. Easy to spot. It has a padded swing door.'

She nodded and went, too shocked to speak. He had been brutal to Irene. Absolutely brutal, and if that had been the keynote to their marriage…

What am I doing? To love a man like this… To love a man who has brought his wife to this…

She found the kitchen, and after a few minutes of searching through its myriad drawers and vast fridge she found a spoon, a glass and juice and brought them back up the stairs to find a different mood now prevailed in the bathroom.

The pills had gone—gathered up and flushed away, probably—and Irene was calm. Almost sheepish, perhaps.

She sat on the edge of the Jacuzzi and Julius sat beside her, holding her gently and saying to her in a voice that betrayed deep warmth and concern, 'For heaven's sake, Irene, if you're going to put on a scene like this, do it for Gary, not for me. I've given you all I can. And all you really want of me, in your heart of hearts. *Accept* that!'

'But do you love me, Julius?' Irene said brokenly.

'Yes, of course I love you,' he answered tightly.

No wonder he'd said to Stevie just six hours ago that they were 'just words'.

She wondered tiredly who Gary could be. Irene's new

boyfriend? It didn't sound as if *that* relationship was working out too well either.

She watched, too drained to think of leaving the room, as Julius pushed the dose of ipecacuanha syrup into Irene's mouth, then they retreated in time to give her privacy as she vomited up the questionable contents of her stomach. Julius just had time to close the bathroom door behind him.

Stevie dreaded being alone with him like this, unable to see either the remotest future to their relationship or how she was going to rid herself of the disease—it felt like a disease, at that moment—of loving him. Fortunately, he didn't give her time to think about it.

'I'm going to call an ambulance,' he said, his care apparent in his voice despite his anger. 'I can't get her to be consistent or coherent about what she's taken. Painkillers, she says, some hours ago, and she's been drinking quite a bit, too. I don't want to risk liver damage, because it's a very real and serious possibility when alcohol and paracetamol are combined at high levels like that. Even if it's nothing, a night in hospital will give her a scare.'

'A *scare*?' Stevie hissed, appalled. 'I never imagined you could be that cruel, Julius! What about her feelings? What about the children?'

'Do you think what she's doing is good for the children?' he bit back. 'If she doesn't accept reality soon, they're going to be damaged permanently. She's trying to convince them of a future that just can't happen, making all of us play impossible roles, and meanwhile the real issues she needs to deal with are being ignored, and soon it will be too late. She talks about divorce, but won't accept that when the divorce settlement is worked out she'll have to leave this house—'

'It's a very nice house,' Stevie drawled, her own sarcasm painful to her.

'But that can't be her major concern!' he rasped hotly. 'And I certainly can't make it a concern of mine! You're obviously sympathetic towards her. I love that warmth in you, Stevie…'

'Don't mention the word "love",' she said through clenched teeth, and saw his eyes blaze.

He quenched the fire quickly and went on, 'But surely you, of all people, wouldn't expect…wouldn't *want*…me to respond to her now…*ever*…simply because that might stop her from losing this *house*?'

'No. No, I wouldn't want that,' she managed thinly, and, though she found the fact appalling, this somehow seemed to satisfy him and he turned from her to reach for the phone by the bed and dial OOO.

'I'll stay here with the children for the rest of the night,' he told Stevie when the call was completed. 'You must take my car and go home. You can drive it to the health centre in the morning, and it'll be there for me at the end of the day. I'll take Lauren to school by taxi and come straight on from there. Kyle can walk. He's at Cranbrook, which is only just up the road.'

'Fine,' she agreed.

She didn't want to hear the details of his children's lives, quite sure that, whatever it cost her in pain and withered hope, she could not respond to him now. She could not go on with this.

It wasn't simply the *fact* of Irene now, and all the emotional complexity that came with her. It was his appalling ability to say I love you, to two different women in one night, while at the same time dismissing the pain of each.

And yet I love him. If I didn't, then this couldn't possibly hurt so much…

'I'm going to tidy up the bathroom before I go,' she told him, her instinct to give coming to the fore again.

If he'd planned to protest, she didn't give him time, and she spent several minutes wiping the blood from the basin, hunting for any pills Julius might have missed and sponging up the streaks of face powder, lipstick and moisturiser which somehow seemed to be spilled and pooled and smeared in several places.

She righted two bottles that still lay on their sides and even polished the mirror, while Irene sat watching her silently.

It was a bizarre scene, and definitely a little theatrical, a little *too* much disorder to be entirely natural since, apart from these very fresh spills, the place was spotless. A professional cleaner had obviously been here within the past twenty-four hours.

Still, was it such a terrible thing to give a cry for help in this way if Irene loved Julius and wanted him back? *Did* she love him? Julius himself had suggested it was just the house...

Irene's thoughts must have been travelling along similar lines.

'Are you serious about Julius?' she suddenly asked.

'No,' Stevie said briefly.

Irene was not satisfied. She added deliberately, 'Because he'll hurt you if you are.'

There wasn't time to say he already had.

Stevie heard an ambulance give a brief whoop of its siren as it pulled up outside the house. Not that she would have admitted her hurt to Irene even if she'd had a chance. It ran too deep for that.

'Are you coming down with Aimee's flu?' asked Ros at work just a few hours later. 'You look rotten.'

Stevie knew that to be true. Her face had stared back at her from the mirror at home this morning white and tightly drawn, with purple shadows painted on the fine skin beneath her brown eyes.

She had driven Julius's car home, as he'd suggested, arriving just after four, and had spend a scant three hours in bed, though to say she had *slept* there would have been an exaggeration. She had just been dozing off at last—a troubled doze, too, with the shapes of ill-omened dreams already gathering on the horizons of her consciousness—when the alarm had gone off and she hadn't dared to ignore it.

If she had failed to arrive some minutes early at the health centre and anyone had seen her at the wheel of Julius's car, she would have faced the necessity of explanations which would have been as easy in her mouth as chewing on nails.

It hadn't happened, though. She'd showered and grabbed the lightest of breakfasts—not hungry, anyway—and had reached work first, now to face this concerned question from Ros.

It would be so easy to take it up and say, yes, she had the flu coming on, so that she would be told to go home again and nurse herself through until the weekend.

She wasn't going to do it, though. Julius had to be faced, and it was better to face him today while anger still had the upper hand over bitter pain.

All along, she thought feverishly, all along, I had doubts. I felt vulnerable, and that things couldn't be as good and as simple as they seemed. And they weren't! Oh, no, they weren't! And then I forgave and I excused and I understood. I worked as hard as I could to understand and forgive, and it still wasn't enough.

There's a point beyond which I can't go, and this is it! I'm not going to take Julius into my life and my heart when it's clear he loves neither me nor Irene enough to do what's right for either of us. Perhaps Irene doesn't have the strength and self-respect to let Julius go, but *I* do! I must!

She managed to fob off Ros's concern with a few words about a bad night. No lies there! Still, Ros talked about sending her home, but Stevie was adamant.

'If I nap during the the day I won't sleep again tonight,' she said firmly. 'I'm tired, yes, but I'll work through it, Ros, and take a good break when the weekend comes. Lizzy in the Kitchen isn't playing this week.'

Which was a pity because, of all things, singing could take her mind off pain. She had learned this in the course of her mother's illness and death, and knew it would be true again now. At least they were scheduled to practise tomorrow night, and that would be nice.

Liz had told Stevie that she wasn't planning to be there so it would be very low-key. She was scheduled for her treatment today. It was a simple matter, just a liquid drink of radioactive iodine, which would shrink the thyroid, while hopefully leaving enough of it to produce the necessary amount of thyroxine. Liz would need a thyroid test at a later date to determine whether the desired result had been achieved. If not, then synthetic thyroxine tablets, taken regularly, would keep her in balance.

She dropped in to say a quick hello to Stevie on her way to Southshore Hospital's Department of Nuclear Medicine. Her brother was with her for transport and emotional support. She looked nervous.

'Dr Marr says it's just a drink and all I have to do is take a deep breath and gulp it down, but... Well, this is stupid. I've always hated taking medicine. I hate the taste, and I have a squeamish stomach when something tastes bad, and what if I gag and retch and just can't get it down and the whole thing is ghastly? I'm sure it must taste terrible!'

'Oh, Liz!' Stevie scolded. 'You're talking yourself into it!'

Liz stared at her for a moment, then gave a sheepish, reluctant grin. 'I am, aren't I? This is what comes of being healthy all my life. When it comes down to it, I'm a great big wuss!'

She left, her resolve more firmly in place.

Julius arrived at nine, just in time to take on his first appointment but with no time for anything more than the briefest of greetings to Stevie. He looked as tired and wrung out as she felt, with the complexity of his concerns etched clearly in the way he held his face and body—shoulders hard and tight, hands clenched, jaw jutting and eyes smouldering.

Stevie had to fight the impulse to let herself quietly into his office before he came out to summon his patient and... What? Yell at him? Or, despite her repudiation of him, tenderly massage the knots from his muscles? She didn't know.

Once this initial impulse had been fought down, however, it was easy to resist for the rest of the morning. There was simply no opportunity once appointments had started.

At lunchtime, however, Julius caught her as she was about to flee the centre. She'd brought sandwiches, and all she intended was to drive to a small park in a side street a few blocks away and eat them there. She probably wouldn't even make the effort to get out of the car!

'Don't you want to know how Irene is?' he challenged, reaching her just seconds before she started her engine.

'Not particularly.' The callous response was merely misplaced bravado on her part, but he was not to know that.

His eyes narrowed. 'Well, I want to tell you,' he growled.

'Go ahead, then,' she offered.

'She's fine. They'll discharge her this morning. There

were no symptoms of liver failure or any other effects from
what she'd taken, other than a bit of dehydration. A hang-
over, basically. But I had to make sure.'

'Of course.'

'Irene has a habit of pulling these sorts of stunts, but it's
like the boy who cried wolf. The one time everyone ignores
it will be the one time it turns out to be real. And at heart
I do—'

'Look,' Stevie interrupted on a hard, strained note, 'do
you really imagine I find it an attractive quality in you, the
way you put down someone who was once such an integral
part—in fact, who still seems to be such an integral part—
of your life? Well, I don't! I find it extremely repellent.
Thank goodness I saw enough of it to end my personal
dealings with you before you started doing the same to me!'

He went white. 'Stevie…'

'Don't try to excuse it.'

'I won't.' His tone was as tight as her own. 'You consider it disloyal to my—'

'"Disloyal" is far too weak a word for it, Julius,' she
told him, then wound up her window, started her engine
and backed out of her parking space before he could react.

He stared after her, with flames of anger and something
else…something too deep to read…doing a warring dance
together in his face.

He came round that night, after an afternoon of huge,
repressed tension on both sides. Stevie wasn't entirely surprised to see him approach up her front path and considered
hiding inside, and not answering the door, but felt that she
owed him *that* much at least.

Standing in the doorway, however, shielding him from
any sight of the house's interior where he had once been
so welcome, she left him in little doubt as to her state
of mind.

'So you won't even *talk* about this?' he rasped at once, anger giving a frightening emphasis to his size and power as a man. She had never felt so hostile towards him…and never been so aware of the male pull he exerted on her female awareness. His scent, the remembered texture of his skin with its mixture of silk and roughness, the taste of him…

'No,' she said. 'It's obvious that I mean it, isn't it? What else could you possibly say when I tell you that I simply won't listen to any "explanations" of yours?'

'And yet last night we made love… You were as tender as a wife the way you cooked for me and woke me in the bath.'

'As tender as a wife? No, thank you!' she commented acidly.

His eyes narrowed and he opened his mouth as if to challenge her statement, but then dismissed it and returned unerringly to his focus.

'We made love, Stevie, and it was wonderful. There was none of this in you then. If Irene's—' He broke off, then went on carefully, 'If her cry for help has changed things between us so irrevocably, then surely I have the right to know how…and why?'

'Haven't I made it clear already? Your response to her showed you in a light I found…just impossible.'

'And yet,' he said quickly, 'if I did what she wanted of me, there'd be no place in my life for you, Stevie. Are you really so very generous?'

'I'm not generous at all when it comes to you.' She laughed harshly. 'I'd have selfishly taken you, and all the emotional baggage you came with, if I'd thought I'd be treated differently to Irene. Last night…no, this morning,' she amended bitterly, 'in those awful wee hours, you showed me that I wouldn't be.'

'You're wrong,' he insisted, the strain in his face showing he was close to breaking point. 'I could say that until the cows come home, but talk is cheap. And you're not going to give me a chance to prove it with action, are you?'

'No, I'm not.'

She expected more from him, but nothing came. His face simply set even harder. It was like grey stone now, and seconds later he turned on his heel and left her verandah, his shoes making a familiar gritty sound on her front path, punctuating the crisp air of the autumn evening.

Shakily, she slipped back into the house and closed the door behind her, then heard his car starting a minute later.

Technically, she supposed, this was her victory. She had got what she wanted—an end to their relationship, and his acceptance of that. She had had the last word. Why, then, did it feel like such a terrible defeat?

CHAPTER TEN

'STEVIE, your voice is really *tight* today!' Alex said accusingly on Thursday night as they sat informally around Stevie's living room, working on the harmonies of two new songs. 'You're not coming down with flu, are you? You look really washed out!'

'If anyone else says that to me, I'll—' Stevie stopped. It was a betrayal of what she felt to get angry at such a well-meant question.

She went on much more carefully, 'No, I'm not getting flu, but I…haven't been sleeping well the past few nights. Backache,' she improvised quickly, and with some truth. 'Sciatic nerve, I think. Possibly being pressured by an impacted disc. Keeps me awake. I must see someone about it soon.'

One thing about working in a health centre, it gave you a wonderful repertoire of plausible medical excuses to use at the drop of a hat. Not prone to dishonesty, Stevie didn't intend to make a habit of it.

'Poor lass!' said Jennie. 'Want to stop? It's not as if we can really get this down in its final form without Liz.'

'How is Liz, anyway, Stevie?' Alison asked. 'Why couldn't she make it tonight?'

'She decided that the thyroid treatment was a good excuse for a much needed break, I think,' Stevie answered. 'And she says she got the radioactive iodine drink down without calamity, which she had been nervous about. I dropped in to her place after work today and found her lolling on the couch, reading a magazine. It's about the first time I've ever seen her in a horizontal position in her own house. Her kids are being great, too. I think it gave them a bit of a scare to find that she wasn't invincible.'

'I'm not surprised,' Jennie said. 'I know nothing about thyroid trouble, Stevie. Is her long-term outlook really as good as she's been told?'

'Apparently, yes. If you're sensible, which Lizzy will be now, I'm sure, you hardly need to remember there was ever a problem. Some people need ongoing thyroid medicine, but Liz won't know for a while if that applies to her. Others need follow-up surgery to reduce an unsightly goitre, but Liz didn't develop one, of course, otherwise she or someone else might have suspected what the problem was much earlier. Or so I've been told. I'm not exactly an expert.'

'But you're thinking of it, aren't you?' Alex came in, direct as usual. 'Isn't that some university course and enrolment information I saw on your kitchen table when I was making the tea?'

Stevie flushed a little. 'I meant to put that away...'

At least Alex hadn't asked about her love life lately!

'Why?' Alex demanded. 'If you're thinking of going back to finish nursing after all this time, I'd be the first to congratulate you and encourage you all the way.'

Alison and Jennie agreed with equal enthusiasm, and Stevie managed to mask her embarrassment. Yes, she had been thinking about getting qualified in nursing or some other area of medicine and health care. She'd sent away for materials from several tertiary institutions, but it still seemed like a private goal, and a fragile one. She was nearly forty. Was it really the time for brave new beginnings?

She had certainly thought so a few weeks ago in her rosy rapture over Julius, but that had turned so miserably, painfully sour. And once before, fifteen years ago, she'd left a

nursing course unfinished. Perhaps that was her destiny—
a life of incompletion, things cut off before they'd had a
chance to flower...

For heaven's sake, stop being so morbid!

She looked around at these three friends of hers and
heard them excitedly sketching out the wide new possibilities in her life.

When she answered them finally, there was a new note
of hope and determination in her voice. 'I'll probably need
your support,' she said, 'because I'll be doing it part time,
and I don't expect study will come easily after all this time.
But, yes, I'm going to try and get into a nursing course
next year.'

'Julius, have you seen it?' Irene's voice squeaked down the
phone at nine on Thursday evening as he sat at home, with
papers covering his desk and turbulent classical music in
the background.

'Seen what, Irene?' He wasn't surprised at her mercurial
change of mood since the other night. She'd been discharged from hospital the previous morning and had
phoned him shortly afterwards to report her intention of
'resting at home'.

He'd approved of it. Despite his simmering anger and
frustration with her, he knew she really did need a break.
A good one.

Now she sounded highly indignant, but there was an underlying excitement to it as well. He knew where this excitement came from, and hoped he hadn't promised her too
much yesterday.

He had reported to her that he'd spoken by phone to Gary
in Perth, and that Gary had been deeply concerned, questioning his own conduct, missing her badly. It was all true.
Gary had used exactly those words. 'Missing her badly.'

But perhaps I shouldn't have told her. If it gives her too much hope and complacency, and she thinks she doesn't have to work at it...

'Seen *what?*' she echoed, and he forced his attention back to the present and to her voice. 'Seen the latest issue of Peter Harkness's journal, of course!'

'No, I haven't,' he answered. 'Why?'

He didn't much like her habit of referring to various world-renowned medical journals in this fashion. Why couldn't she just call them *Lancet* or the *B.M.J.* like everyone else?

Well, he knew why. It was all part of the emotional neediness that sat so much at odds with her brilliant brain. If she happened to know the editor or senior staff journalist of a certain publication personally, then that publication was inevitably 'Peter's' or 'Kate's' or 'Russell's' from then on.

'*Because,*' she went on, 'some snotty little doctor from some awful American university has completely pre-empted our work, and published this month. *That's* why!'

Julius experienced one pang of panic, then remembered who he was talking to and said patiently, 'Start at the beginning, Irene. With details. Pre-empted what, exactly?'

It took several minutes to get the full story, during which time he'd rummaged through his pile of unopened mail, found the journal in question and the article she was talking about and had managed to skim through it, with Irene dictating page numbers and paragraphs to him.

As usual she had exaggerated vastly. Yes, there was a good deal of overlap in this unknown Dr Morton Nederlander's area of research, and he'd reached the same conclusion, in the same area, that Julius and Irene had been working towards for so long, but it wasn't really bad news...

In fact, it was the best news he'd heard in a long time. His mind raced ahead. This actually took the pressure off to a huge degree. Dr Nederlander had published first. Great! There was absolutely no point in trying for the journal's next deadline now, as Irene had kept insisting on.

Indeed, it would be far better to present their own research findings as an answer to Dr Nederlander's, which meant they had months, not weeks, to get the work done, and he could relax, live like a human being again, take on what should have been his role with his former research partner for the past two months—that of consultant on the final drafts, instead of shouldering the lion's share of the writing himself.

The sense of lifted pressure was enormous and exhilarating and wonderful…until he remembered Stevie. She had made it painfully apparent yesterday that she considered their relationship over. Irrevocably over. Was he going to accept that? Or would he fight it with everything he had?

'Are you sure you should be back at work, Aimee?' said Dr Rebecca Irwin, then held a steaming mug of morning coffee to her lips.

'It's my last day, Dr Irwin. How could I possibly stay away and miss this gathering? Anyway, I'm feeling much better—though admittedly under the influence of pills!'

'Oh, for heaven's sake, I didn't mean you had to stay away altogether!' the dark and attractive young doctor scolded Aimee. 'But I'm sure Ros would have forgiven you if you'd just turned up for our farewell breakfast and then gone home again.'

All the health centre's staff were gathered in the reception area just before opening hours, enjoying a special breakfast of fruit salad and croissants to wish Aimee Hilliard and Rebecca Irwin well.

Rebecca was finishing at the health centre today, too, after filling in here part time on a shifting schedule of hours for several months. Her father's practice was expanding now, and she would be needed there full time soon.

'My only real doubt about coming in was that you might catch my flu,' Aimee said to the vibrant young doctor. 'I'd hate to be responsible for spoiling your wedding tomorrow!'

Dr Irwin blushed frankly. 'I'm not sure that anything could do that!' she said. 'Unless Harry and I have a big fight, I suppose...'

'Can't imagine you have many of those, Rebecca,' came in Gareth Searle, the health centre's director as well as being an old friend of Rebecca's father.

'Can't you just?' she retorted with spirit. 'Wrong! We have them all the time! Very, very nice fights, actually...'

She gave a smile that managed to be both wicked and dreamy at the same time, then went on, 'No, but, as far as me getting sick goes, I have been crossing my fingers that no patients sneeze on me today. Still, we're taking a four-week honeymoon, with good locums in place to help Dad and Grace, so we couldn't possibly *both* be sick for *all* of it!'

'Where are you going, Rebecca?' It was Julius.

'Europe. Neither of us have been before. We didn't think we could manage four weeks, but Dad is insisting. Can't wait, I must say. You must have some recommendations, Julius, about what to see?'

Stevie wished she weren't standing in this particular circle of conversation. She hadn't contributed for the past few minutes so she could easily have slipped back to the health centre's kitchen to get another croissant or some more coffee, but she'd left it too late, enjoying hearing about Ros's and Aimee's plans. And now Julius had joined them...

He looked different today, she realised. Less fatigued. Less stressed. And with a sizzling aura of determination about him.

She hated the way she was so aware of him, and so sensitive to those subtle changes. Her gaze kept tangling with his, and she hated that too. On Wednesday he had seemed to accept what she'd told him about how she felt. Today, she sensed that he was out for a battle.

'I'm not the source you're looking for, Rebecca,' he was saying, cheerfully rueful. 'My expertise on Europe consists of being able to compare conference facilities in Amsterdam, Milan, Edinburgh and Bordeaux.'

'You've never been to Paris?'

'Two hours in transit at Orly airport.'

'Or London?'

'That conference was cancelled.'

'Or Tuscany?'

'The view from the plane window was obscured by cloud, I was told, but I was reading a medical journal anyway.'

Rebecca laughed. 'You're amazing, Julius!'

'Because I haven't seen Europe properly?'

'Because you don't seem to mind.'

'I don't,' he said.

'And you seem to almost be laughing at your former self.'

'I am. There's a lot to laugh at. And there's plenty of time to see Europe. I'll do it soon.'

'Will you?'

'Maybe.' He shrugged cheerfully, as if it didn't matter at all, then said very casually, 'Stevie, can I see you in my office for a moment?'

He had caught her so totally off guard that she'd agreed before even remembering that the option of 'No' existed, and he'd been so off-hand about it that no one else seemed to read anything into it. And perhaps they were right, and it was something trivial about the workday ahead.

Only somehow she knew it was not.

Just a few moments later they were alone, with the door carefully shut behind him.

She stood stiffly, waiting, without the slightest idea what it could be about.

'Look,' he said, 'this won't take long. I just wanted to share some good news with you.'

There was a tiny pause, as if he was waiting for her to say something, but she didn't...couldn't...so he went on with a sudden change of mood. 'Oh, Stevie, I don't know if this will mean anything to you. I hope it will. I—I doubt if you can understand how much I hope so. I had some news last night which really takes the pressure off my workload now, and it should make the situation with Irene improve enormously. I'm not sure if she's seen that yet, but she will. And I've spoken to Gary. He was very concerned to hear about her behaviour lately, and he's been rethinking things on his own as well. I wouldn't be surprised if—' He stopped and then continued impotently, 'But that's irrelevant to you and me.'

'Julius, there *is* no you and me,' Stevie pointed out in a hard little voice. 'Haven't we been through this?'

She could see the way he had to physically bite back an urgent contradiction. The muscles at his jaw were bunched, and anyone who had ever called him loose-limbed couldn't possibly have done so now.

'All right,' he said. 'This isn't the time or the place.'

'Then I'll leave, if you don't mind. I have work to do.'

'Go ahead. I'd hoped you'd share a little of my pleasure that pressures have eased, that's all.'

'Oh, I do. I do,' she answered, wondering how it was

possible that she still cared like this. The sight of the new energy and purpose in him was precious to her, despite everything.

They both got through the morning somehow. It was busy, with an underlying sense of excitement and change coming at Stevie, it seemed, from all sides. Rebecca was in a mood of electric happiness and anticipation. Running late, too, as she had to take three phone calls during the morning about wedding arrangements.

It was to be an intimate ceremony and reception. 'But somehow that doesn't make it any simpler,' she groaned to Stevie at one point. 'What on earth made us think we wanted a string quartet?'

'I'm sorry Rebecca will be away on her honeymoon for my first four weeks in the new practice,' Aimee said a little later. 'Going through the routine here for the last time, I can't help wondering how different it will be. I hope I'm not nervous on Monday.'

'I can't imagine you're ever nervous, Aimee,' Stevie told the older woman truthfully. 'You always seem so unflappable.'

'Oh, you'd be surprised…'

Then, just as Stevie was about to go to lunch at one, a comfortably padded blonde in very percussive high heels walked through the front door, and she recognised Irene.

Fortunately Ros Reynolds was at the front desk at that moment, and it was apparent that the two women hadn't met so there was no tension.

'Hello,' Ros said, with her usual polite and efficient good cheer. 'Are you here for an appointment?'

'Of sorts, yes.' Irene smiled confidently. 'I'm here to see Julius for lunch.'

'And he's expecting you?'

'Yes. I'm his former research partner from the university.' Irene caught sight of Stevie, who was entering the reception area with an ungainly stack of patient files in her hands, and added deliberately, 'Although I hope soon to say I'm his fiancée.'

'Oh. Well. Congratulations,' Ros murmured, taken aback by this apparently gratuitous confession. Or was it an announcement? Ros evidently decided to take it that way, and added with more enthusiasm, 'I hope you'll both be very happy…'

'Irene!' Julius strode forward, concealing his anger.

Until he'd spoken, he knew Stevie hadn't seen his approach from his office along the corridor, but he'd had plenty of opportunity to hear Irene's words and see their effect on her. She looked stricken, stone-faced…yet confused rather than surprised.

Like someone… He struggled for an apt comparison, and after a few seconds it came to him. She looked like a boxer who was expecting a blow to the jaw and got one in the stomach instead.

She had expected the pain, in other words. She just hadn't expected the direction it came from. What on earth did she think about Irene? It didn't make sense…but at last it was starting to.

If he'd been a violent man, he could have shaken Irene. His fiancée? Hadn't she realised yet that marriage to him was the last thing she really wanted?

Evidently not. She was the type of woman who needed a man the way she needed oxygen, and the necessity of seeing their years of research together finally come to fruition had kept him at her beck and call long after he would, in any other situation, have tactfully removed himself from her life—more for her own good than for his.

Last night he'd brought her round to his way of thinking on the issue of Morton Nederlander publishing his findings first, and she'd suggested lunch. 'To celebrate the lifting of the load.' Since it was exactly what he felt like celebrating—perhaps the only thing he felt like celebrating in his life at the moment—he'd agreed.

But he wouldn't have agreed if he'd known she was going to come in here and deliberately give Stevie such a mistaken impression of their relationship.

Except that it's not new to her, he realised, thinking again of Stevie's expression. She really does think we have some huge, intimate connection. What exactly does she think? And why?

He wondered, with a degree of desperation, what this week was doing to his blood pressure.

Irene was waiting for him. He wanted to talk to her urgently and seriously about Gary. He couldn't have things out with Stevie now. When could he? Never, if she wouldn't let him.

Surely it couldn't come to that, he thought in anguish as he said aloud to Irene, 'Let's go. I can't take more than an hour, and there's a lot to say.'

'You *are* coming down with my flu, aren't you?' Aimee said to Stevie when Julius's hour was almost up.

Did that make the sixth time someone had asked her that this past week? Stevie wondered. Maybe the seventh. 'Well, I—' she began.

'Go home,' Aimee urged. 'Whatever it is, it's something, and you need to give in to it and rest.'

'Would you be able to manage?'

'Of course. Anna might be able to come in. She never minds a few extra hours, now that she has a mortgage.'

'OK, then…' Since Stevie had a pounding headache, no appetite and felt quite dizzy from stress and sleeplessness, it was probably more responsible to go home.

An hour later she was lying on her bed with the windows shaded, waiting for two headache tablets to take effect and wishing that certain other less physical pains had as easy and rapid a cure. Without meaning to at all, she slept...

To wake with heavy limbs and a groggy brain hours later at the sound of a persistent hammering on the front door. In a daze, she got herself down the passage and answered it, too woolly-witted even to wonder about who it might be.

Julius.

'Aimee said you'd gone home with flu.' He strode into the house without giving her time to think of shutting the door. In his face? Might she have reached that point if she'd been thoroughly awake?

'I think it was just a migraine. I'm feeling much better now,' she told him.

'You don't look it,' he accused gently.

'I've been asleep.'

'You still are, aren't you?'

'I'll be all right in a minute,' she insisted.

'Freshen up in the bathroom while I get you something to drink. Tea? Or one of those cool, dry gin and tonics of yours?'

'Tea, please,' she said quickly. She didn't need anything even mildly alcoholic to fuel the heat and anger between them.

A vigorous splash of her face and some cold mouthfuls of water brought alertness but no lessening of stress. When she reached the kitchen her heart lurched at the way Julius seemed so familiar and at home here.

It was getting dark and he'd switched on the two old-fashioned ceiling lights with their fluted glass shades. Now he was pouring boiling water into Mum's old china teapot, with the pattern of yellow and pink roses. He was too masculine a man for such a pretty, feminine kitchen, and yet he belonged. He'd even found the knitted cosy, the strainer, the milk and the cups.

And he was smiling at her. That wide, slow smile she loved. It was tinged with something, though... Vulnerability. The fact that he dared to let it show threatened to rob her of the only thing that could keep her strength up in his presence—her anger.

'Julius,' she said desperately, 'if there's a good reason why you've come, then tell me it now, straight out. If there isn't, please, leave!'

'Milk?'

She ignored him. 'And *don't*...please, don't...try and play games with your words.'

He abandoned the tea and came towards her. She stood her ground, thinking, If he's under the impression he can seduce me out of this talk, then he can think again.

'There are no games, Stevie,' he said, his low voice catching on her name. 'But I realised today that you had utterly the wrong idea about me and Irene.'

'I—'

'Don't! Let me say it.' He was standing very close, but hadn't tried to touch her. 'You think I'm the father of her children, don't you? That we've been in some kind of a relationship for years. She admitted to me today that she'd deliberately given you that impression on the phone two weeks ago, and, heaven knows, it wouldn't have been hard to make it credible in view of how closely we've been connected.'

'So you admit that—'

'I'm not admitting anything,' he ground out, shifting his weight angrily. 'Let me say it! *All* of it!'

'A-all right.'

'Irene and I were research partners for twelve years.'

'I realise that now,' she said with heavy patience. 'Are you saying that's the only way in which you were close?'

'No! Of course I'm not!' he rasped. 'I was in love with her…thought I was…for nearly seven years! And she knew it, too, although I was too wrapped up in science and medicine to see that then.'

'I don't quite understand.'

'From the beginning, Stevie, she was married to Gary, who was and is a wealthy and successful businessman and a very nice human being.' His voice was low and rapid, as if he was impatient with the length and complexity of what he had to say. 'She loved him too—still does—but made the fatal mistake of taking him for granted and trying to keep me on a string as well.'

'I can't imagine you on anyone's string, Julius,' Stevie blurted, her eyes narrowed as she tried to read everything about his tone and his body language.

'I've changed,' he said. 'Back then I was the archetypal scientist in so many ways, completely focused on my work, with no time to give to developing myself in other areas. Women were an alien species to me. My private life didn't exist. Irene and I related very well over our work. She's very bright, despite her flaws of character.' He gave a faint, rueful smile. 'It was very easy for her to wind me around her finger and keep me there. Easy, and useful, too. She needs people to lean on, needs adoration. And I gave it to her.'

'You had an affair.' She had to say it that bluntly, for her own protection.

He flinched and stiffened. 'Never, Stevie! Never that!' Then he touched her at last, taking the softness of her upper arms in a commanding yet caressing grip. 'For one thing, I was too naïve, sexually, in my twenties, to believe that she'd betray her husband. I never touched her. Oh, she touched me.' Again that rueful, complex smile. 'Just enough to keep my senses aflame without me even realising it was deliberate. Then gradually…I don't know how it happened. I matured, I suppose. And I lost my parents. I did a lot of soul-searching… The balance in my relationship with Irene changed.'

His arms had closed around Stevie now, and she was gazing up into his face, just listening, taking it in, not reacting yet. But loving his touch and his warmth and his scent, heaven help her…

'I still respected her mind and her research,' he went on. 'As I still do. But I started questioning my life and what I was doing with it, and realised that I wasn't happy. I didn't like who I was, spending every waking moment at the university and coming home to a ghastly little flat which Irene quite rightly ridiculed.'

'Ridiculed?'

'Cramped, ugly, the bare bones of furniture, just a clutter of books and papers, and never anything in the fridge. Back then I barely noticed. I was too busy with my work, and venting my emotional needs in longing for a woman who was not only unattainable but, I found in the end, not who I'd thought she was, and not what I wanted. It all came to a head about three years ago.'

'Irene left her husband…'

'No! I decided to get out of the research scene, get back to the grass roots of medicine and, I hoped, to the grass roots of myself and what was important to me. I did a refresher course and became a GP. Professionally, you know the rest. The only problem was, there was a huge comparative study that Irene and I had undertaken which wasn't completed. I couldn't abandon our work on that, and yet I hated the thought of waiting until we could do the follow-up surveys last year which would make the whole thing fall into place and give us our results.

'Irene urged me to follow my instincts about my own future and leave the research scene. In that she was very generous. All she wanted, she said at the time, was for me to help with the final task of turning our findings into a number of different research papers, do some of the statistical work on the computer, run my eye over the drafts of the papers she would be writing up. I'm sure she meant it at the time, too. After all, my dropping out would give her the lion's share of the credit, although I'm not saying that was her only reason. She's not a bad person.

'But then, over this past Christmas, her marriage to Gary broke down. I didn't know why until last night when I talked to him. He's been in Perth. She had an affair with her new research assistant. To put it cynically, I imagine she couldn't keep that particular man dangling without a full-on seduction.' This time his smile was harder, less tender. 'But, of course, it didn't last, she lost the assistant and Gary found out, and he's a principled man who cares for Irene very much. He was hurt and angry, and he had a big project to oversee in Perth so he used that as a way to separate.'

'And divorce, presumably? Irene seems to want that.'

'She doesn't. Not at all. But it's taken her months to see it. I actually wanted to bully her into it the other night when she tried that dramatic trick with the pills.'

'I remember now.' Stevie nodded. 'You said she should be putting on the performance for Gary, not you. That didn't make any sense to me then.'

'And I was right. Fortunately, I know Gary is prepared to give her another chance now, and he's due back from Perth today. The problem was that Irene panicked at first and turned to me—partly because she'd been used to taking me for granted in that way for so long years ago, and partly because she just couldn't focus on her work in her emotional state. It's been—'

He broke off and sighed, let Stevie go, turned restlessly and ran a tense hand up through his dark hair. Pacing, then turning back to her, he said, 'I've hated it, Stevie, but there was no way out of it. Our research was ultimately too important to let it slide, and we were so close to completing the whole thing. If she'd abandoned it and had a breakdown, which she was close to, I think... And, personally, I didn't want to let her down. Or Gary and the children. I'm Kyle's godfather, and I've known them since they were born.'

'But why didn't you tell me all of this from the beginning?'

'I should have,' he said harshly, his body held tightly now so that she wanted to go up to him and massage the tension of self-reproach away. 'I understood that very strongly the moment I saw you there on the stage at Lauren's school fête. As to why I didn't... Perhaps I was ashamed.'

'*Ashamed?* Of *what*, Julius?' She stepped towards him. 'It seems to me you've been quite heroic in your willingness to help Irene, and surely you can see that I would have understood that if I'd known about it...if I hadn't been left to put it together so wrongly!'

'But I hated the fact that I'd been so wrong, myself, about what I felt for Irene for so many years. And what I felt for you...what I *feel*...' he looked up into her face, his slate-grey eyes smoking with need '...is so precious and so right, Stevie, I just wanted to keep you out of that whole mess. What we had was so new. I didn't trust that you'd be able to forgive the complexity of my relationship with Irene.'

'Why, Julius?'

'Why?' he rasped. 'Stevie, how could I expect my new, wonderful lover to understand that I *wasn't* interested in this woman who was blatantly trying to get me into her bed, who was taking hours of my time every week and who was demanding that I fill in as a male role model for the absent father of her children? But I was wrong. I should have been honest with you.'

'Yes, you should,' she agreed quietly.

He was silent, pacing the room again. His back was to her now, but his voice carried clearly as he asked, 'Then it's too late? You can't forgive my mistake?'

'Oh, Julius, no! I can't forgive *mine*!' she told him, her voice cracking. 'You were wrong at first, yes, but it was a very human mistake and I was doubly wrong later when I insisted that I knew what was going on and wouldn't let you explain. I—I should have listened to you, trusted that there was more.'

'And I thought you did know it all,' he said. 'You told me you'd talked to Irene.'

'She'd said she was your partner.'

'Deliberately trading on the modern ambiguity in that word,' he said slowly.

'Yes, but my imagination did the rest.'

'Your imagination had plenty of fuel.' He faced her, then spread his lean hands in a gesture of helplessness and appeal. 'I love you, Stevie. And I know what the word means now, in a way that I didn't at all when I was in my twenties and so naïvely infatuated with Irene. Please, tell me that we can get past this!'

It would have been so easy to give in completely to his open, hoarse-voiced appeal, but she made herself stay firm for just a little longer.

'To what, Julius?' She knew what she wanted, the only

thing that would satisfy her now after so many weeks of doubt and pain, but wanted to hear him say it. A part of her was still terrified that he wouldn't.

There was a silence, and the space that separated them— just a few feet of it—seemed like solid matter. But she wasn't going to touch him yet. Finally, without taking his eyes off her face, he said it.

'To marriage. It's very simple in the end. I want to marry you, Stevie. I have since that first night we spent together. Probably longer. I want the completeness of it, the statement of trust, the public commitment, our lives woven together. I just want you…us…and if I can't have that—' He broke off and shook his head, as if unwilling to put into words what that loss would mean to him. Fortunately, he didn't have to.

'You *can* have it, Julius,' she whispered. 'With all my heart, and for ever. If I hadn't felt this way about you, nothing that went on between you and Irene would have had the power to hurt me as it did. It was only because it mattered so much that I cut you off the way I did, turned it into such a huge issue in my heart and mind. Does that make sense?'

'Absolute sense,' he said. 'Complete, utter, wonderful sense, my darling woman.' Then he added, as he took her confidently into his arms, 'I think almost everything is going to make that kind of sense for the two of us from now on…'

And if his kiss…long, sweet, teasing…was anything to go by, then he was quite right.

A FAMILY TO CARE FOR by Judy Campbell

Dr Sally Jones isn't quite sure what she wants next, so the locum post at the general practice in the Scottish Highlands will give her time to decide. Finding widowed Dr Rob Mackay there is not altogether a pleasant surprise, because he'd walked out on her in the past. This Rob is more serious, and the father of toddler twin boys, yet he attracts her as strongly as ever...

POTENTIAL HUSBAND by Lucy Clark
A follow on to Potential Daddy

When rural GP Vicky Hansen first met orthopaedic surgeon Steven Pearce, she was deeply attracted, but resigned to him returning to the city—until she found he'd bought some of her family land to renovate the cottage there. Meanwhile, he says, he will be her lodger!

FOR JODIE'S SAKE by Maggie Kingsley

Widowed for two years, Kate Rendall wants to start afresh, and takes the job offered by widower Dr Ethan Flett to care for his fourteen year old daughter, Jodie. Kate is shocked by the instant attraction she feels for Ethan, which is mutual, but while Jodie might like Kate as a carer, would she accept her as a mother?

MILLS & BOON®

⊣ͱ MEDICAL
ROMANCE™

DEFINITELY DADDY by Alison Roberts

Going back to work was exciting and hard for Harriet
McKinlay. It meant putting her adored almost three year
old, Freddie, in nursery. But why did the spinal unit boss,
Patrick Miller, dislike her? She didn't know that Paddy had
saved her life when she gave birth, or that he had the
wrong idea about her morals!

TENDER LOVING CARE by Jennifer Taylor
Dalverston General Hospital

Midwife Sarah Harris had devoted herself to work, but the
arrival of Dr Niall Gillespie, as new head of the department,
changed all that. Except that Niall held everyone at bay—
could she break down the barriers he had so carefully
erected?

ONCE A WISH by Carol Wood
The first of two books

Dr Alissa Leigh, widowed with a small daughter, has been
working at the health centre for a while when Dr Max
Darvill and his son arrive. But Max's ex-wife is still very
visible, and despite the friendship of the two children, Alissa
isn't convinced that Max is really free to love her...

Available from 7th April 2000

*Available at most branches of WH Smith, Tesco,
Martins, Borders, Easons, Volume One/James Thin
and most good paperback bookshops*

0003/03

FREE

4 BOOKS
AND A SURPRISE GIFT!

We would like to take this opportunity to thank you for reading this Mills & Boon® book by offering you the chance to take FOUR more specially selected titles from the Medical Romance™ series absolutely FREE! We're also making this offer to introduce you to the benefits of the Reader Service™—

    ★ FREE home delivery   ★ FREE gifts and competitions
    ★ FREE monthly Newsletter   ★ Exclusive Reader Service discounts
        ★ Books available before they're in the shops

Accepting these FREE books and gift places you under no obligation to buy; you may cancel at any time, even after receiving your free shipment. Simply complete your details below and return the entire page to the address below. **You don't even need a stamp!**

YES! Please send me 4 free Medical Romance books and a surprise gift. I understand that unless you hear from me, I will receive 6 superb new titles every month for just £2.40 each, postage and packing free. I am under no obligation to purchase any books and may cancel my subscription at any time. The free books and gift will be mine to keep in any case.

MOEC

Ms/Mrs/Miss/Mr ....Initials ....
                                                                    BLOCK CAPITALS PLEASE

Surname ....

Address ....

....

....Postcode ....

Send this whole page to:
UK: FREEPOST CN81, Croydon, CR9 3WZ
EIRE: PO Box 4546, Kilcock, County Kildare (stamp required)